# YOU DON'T
# HAVE TO
# BE A
# PERFECT
# GIRL

# YOU DON'T HAVE TO BE A PERFECT GIRL

**Patricia Aks**

SCHOLASTIC BOOK SERVICES
New York Toronto London Auckland Sydney Tokyo

ISBN 0-590-31397-5

12 11 10 9 8 7 6 5 4 3 2 1          1          1 2 3 4 5 6/8

*To my sister*

*Special thanks to Carol Elsner,
who was exceedingly generous
with her time, her expertise,
and her gymnasts.*

# I _____

"Elizabeth, honey, we're going now. You're sure you don't want to come along?" It was my mother asking me if I didn't want to go shopping with her and my sister Carolyn.

"No, thanks," I said. "I'm going to help Daddy with the furniture." I tried not to sound annoyed, but every Saturday my mother, Emma Jean, wants me to go shopping with her and Carolyn, and every Saturday I refuse. Today I had a real excuse, but if I didn't, I'm pretty good at manufacturing one. It's not that I really lie, but I don't want to get into a hassle with my mother and Carolyn if I can avoid it.

Then I heard Carolyn saying, "If I see some red hot T-shirts or some jeans with bells, I'll bring them home for you."

I wasn't sure if she was being sarcastic or not, so I just said, "Thanks a lot. See ya later."

I heard the door slam and I heaved a sigh of relief. It was almost ten o'clock, and I was alone in the house. My father had left for the paint store and was going to bring back sandpaper, a walnut stain, and varnish, so we could refinish an old table he'd picked up at a flea market in upstate New York the week before.

Refinishing furniture is one of my father's favorite forms of relaxation, even though it's hard work, and I love to help him. It takes a lot of elbow grease, but my father says using his muscles on weekends relaxes his brain, which is overworked all week. He's a research chemist in a big firm in Westchester, and although he keeps regular hours, he has a lot of paper work at home, and in his free time he likes to do something physical. I'm with him! School's okay, and I manage to get good grades without exactly killing myself, but I like being physically active on the weekends too. Shopping, for me, is endsville.

Not so for Carolyn. Shopping and boys are her things in life. She's seventeen — only two years older than me — but we might as well be light years apart. She could be my mother's clone, they're so much alike in looks and in taste. They both have blond hair, which Carolyn wears to her shoulder; cat-green eyes; and hourglass figures. They are pretty, but personally I think that are too preoccupied with their looks. All my friends say how attractive and young-looking Emma Jean is, and I agree. And I suppose if you've heard that all your life, looks can't help but have priority over a lot of other things.

I know that Emma Jean really does love me, but we're on such different wavelengths I sometimes can't believe she's really my mother. In fact, when I was about eight years old, I wondered if I was adopted. After all, Carolyn and Emma Jean looked and acted exactly alike, and I felt left out. Even then, they could chatter about clothes. I can still remember one time around Christmas when my grandmother on my mother's side, who still lives in Atlanta, Georgia, where my mother was born and raised, sent her usual check to buy "party dresses" for the girls. There was this big discussion that went on for days between my mother and sister about whether Carolyn should get the green velvet with a lace collar or the red velvet with buttons. Whichever they decided on, I would get the same, two sizes smaller. The fact that my opinion wasn't sought didn't bother me at all. I couldn't believe anything so insignificant could occupy so much time.

Now I realize that they enjoyed talking about clothes, and in fact, Carolyn wants to be a clothes designer. I respect her for that. I guess everyone has to do their own thing, and it's not fair for me to pass judgment.

The problem is that sometimes they make me feel weird because I'm so out of their orbit. That's why when I was little I used to fantasize that the babies were mixed up in the hospital and I belonged to a different mother. Except I knew even when I was a little kid that I did belong to my father. And *we* look alike. We both have light-brown hair, and I occassionally wear mine in a pony tail. Also, my father and I have slightly pointed noses, hazel-colored eyes that change with the weather, and identical dimples that show on the right side of our faces when we smile.

My mother once commented that I was the image of my father from the day I was born. Then she giggled, "I don't know what part I played." She never had to wonder about Carolyn's maternity.

Carolyn and I were always different. When we were little, I preferred stuffed animals to playing with dolls. Carolyn could sit for hours changing her doll's clothes, having tea parties for them, rearranging the furniture in her dollhouse. My mother would encourage me to join in on rainy afternoons when I was forced to stay indoors, but I was more interested in my stuffed animals. I had a complete menagerie by the time I was six years old, and my father constructed an animal house for me. While Carolyn was playing house I was playing zookeeper.

Whenever it was possible, I played outside, and climbing trees was one of my favorite occupations. We have a huge oak in our backyard, and I managed to squiggle up and sit in the lower branches.

Emma Jean, who often watched me from the kitchen window, would say in a loud voice to my father, "John, that child is going to give me cardiac arrest."

My father always defended me. "She knows what she's doing. Leave her alone."

"Well, thank goodness there's only *one* tomboy in the family," my mother would add.

I used to resent being called a tomboy, but then I got used to it. I guess you can get accustomed to a lot of things you don't like — or at least build up an immunity. For example, it bugged me that my mother and Carolyn call me Elizabeth. Everyone else calls me Liz. But my mother insists that Elizabeth Franklin is such a lovely name, it's a shame not to use it, and now I would think it was strange if she called me anything else.

# 2 _____

I try to understand my mother's hang-ups. In fact, I wrote a paper about her in my Human Relations class. Human Relations is one of those experimental courses that is offered in my school, and it's not required, but my best friend, Tracy Brimshaw, and I decided to enroll. Our other closest friends, Jackie and Ellen, thought we were crazy to take anything that wasn't required, but we thought it would be fun. We were right. It's turning out to be one of the best and strangest courses I've ever had.

Our teacher, Ms. Nelson, treats us more like friends than students. The first day of class she explained that she would like us to call her by her first name, Jane, but that the principal, Mr. Jasper, would not approve, and then she added that it's worthwhile to bend on the small issues in order to win the big ones.

Ms. Nelson has just graduated from Teacher's College and she does seem closer to our age than any of my other teachers, but she's already earned our respect. School started the first week in September and it's not even Halloween yet, but I'm already hoping I can take her course next semester. There's so much talk about her course now that everyone is dying to get into it.

She has a way of making the material really meaningful. For example, she tried to make the point that personal values are formed as a result of family tradition and made us see how rebellion can be traced to background. In other words, people have to rebel against something. The conclusion was we can't ever escape the way we are raised.

Last week she asked us to choose a person we know well and write a profile explaining that person's character through his or her heritage. She promised that the paper would be confidential, if that's what we wanted, but that the point was to understand why people behave in certain ways.

I chose my mother as a subject, and I was amazed at how much insight I gained even though it doesn't seem to help much when she doesn't understand me. I mean she isn't even in favor of the ERA! She thinks it puts down homemakers. I don't know yet what I want to do in life, but I know it will be something in addition to keeping house. When I said that to my mother she said, "Elizabeth, honey, why work if you don't have to?"

I could have given her a million reasons, but I don't think it would matter. She just doesn't understand. Maybe it would help if she wrote a profile on me.

I can see things more clearly about her now

that I've got them down in black and white. It's obvious that she never recovered from being an old-fashioned Southern belle. I can almost see her in a beautiful white dress, entertaining her beaus on the porch of the old Georgian mansion where she was born and lived all her life.

We visit my grandmother once a year in Atlanta. I don't know what my grandfather was like because he died the year I was born, but Granny is almost a caricature of the Southern grande dame. I love her, and I think she's funny, and she thinks that anything or anyone who belongs to her is perfect — even my father, even though he's not exactly her type. Granny never fails to tell me that "Emma Jean was the prettiest and most popular girl in town. She could have had anyone."

I always take that as a crack at my father who met my mother when he was on a scholarship at Duke University. He was visiting his roommate one Christmas holiday and met my mother at a dance. According to Emma Jean, it was love at first sight. I get the sense from Granny that she didn't consider John a "catch." According to Granny a "catch" is Eastern Establishment Ivy League and Rich, or else someone descended from a Good Old Southern Family and Rich. Since my father was neither Establishment or Southern, and was definitely poor, it must have been difficult for her to be overjoyed at her daughter's choice. But Emma Jean was determined, and I think that's one quality I've inherited from her, and even Granny had to admit that John had good looks and a quiet charm that was quite irresistible. So even though Emma Jean and John are so different, they rarely fight. They both love the house, which is a split-level ranch on a shady street in what can only be described as a typical suburban block. My mother is constantly redecorating. She just made new curtains for her bedroom, and my father's latest project was to lay new tile in the downstairs bathroom.

"Your father's the cleverest man I know," my mother exclaimed when she saw the results, which were very professional.

My father looked pleased and said, "And think of the money we saved!"

So, generally, things are not bad around here. And I know I shouldn't complain. Somewhere I know, too, that I can always count on Emma Jean and Carolyn, and there's no question that I'm "Daddy's girl."

# 3

I was upstairs, shoveling out my room, which is what I always do on Saturday. I have twin beds, but by the end of the week, one of them is piled up with so much junk that I can hardly see it. My mother nagged me about it daily. Finally my father suggested that I neaten it to "West Point inspection perfect" one day a week, and the rest of the time keep it as messy as I want. Emma Jean agreed, and I do try to keep up my half of the bargain.

Carolyn's room, of course, is always perfect.

I was almost done putting away my clothes when I heard my father come into the house. The first thing he did was call upstairs. "I'm home, Lizo. C'mon down."

"Coming," I yelled back, and leapt down the stairs, two at a time.

My father was already bringing the old painted table out of the storage space in the garage when I arrived in the yard.

"Grab the bundles from the car. We can start right in."

"Sure," I said, and opened the door to the car that was parked in the driveway. I took out a shopping bag that said "Miller's Hardware," and spread the contents on the lawn. Then I read the instructions that were on one of the cans. First we had to apply the paint remover, then wait a few minutes, scrape the surface, let that dry, and start sanding.

We have a flagstone patio and my father had dragged the table into the center. "Better spread some newspapers under here or your mother will have our heads."

"You're right." I laughed and wondered why I felt so conspiratorial as I went into the back door and down the stairs to the cellar where we have a washing machine and drier. We also keep a stack of old newspapers there for my father's various projects.

I picked up a pile of papers and brought them back up the cellar stairs.

"Slide some under here," my father said as he tipped the table. I followed his instructions and then spread some more papers around the edges.

Just then Tracy whizzed into the backyard. "Hiya," she greeted us as she slid off her bicycle. Then flashing us her toothpaste smile, and pointing to her teeth, she beamed, "Look, Ma, no cavities."

"Congratulations! Glad you made it." Tracy had promised to come over after her dentist appointment, if it wasn't too late.

"You're just on time and exactly what we needed," my father said. "I have two brushes and you can use mine to apply the paint remover. I'll just sit back and make sure you're doing it right, in between reading my newspaper."

"Terrific, J.," Tracy said gleefully. She can't quite bring herself to call my father John, so she calls him by his initial. And she calls my mother E.J. I'm not sure my mother approves but I know she likes Tracy, even though by Southern standards she may seem a little fresh.

My mother forgives her because Tracy's father left her mother when she was only two years old, and neither Tracy nor her mother has seen him since.

"That Tracy Nearing's remarkable, considering her background," Emma Jean once remarked to my father when she didn't know I was listening.

"Maybe that's why she's remarkable," my father observed.

There was a brief silence, and then my mother said thoughtfully, "Maybe."

I had to smile at her response, because even though E.J.'s snobbery surfaces sometimes, she will listen to reason and my father in his quiet way calls the shots.

Tracy's mother is a supervising nurse in the Westchester Hospital and her hours are very irregular. That means Tracy is alone a lot, but she takes it in stride. At least she seems to. One thing is for sure, and that's that she's more fun to be with than almost anybody I know.

She never talks about her father, but I think she must miss having a man around the house. Once she confided to me that she wished her mother, who is very nice but super efficient, would remarry.

"I think she's afraid of men," Tracy told me one time when she spent an overnight at my house and we talked until three in the morning.

"Can't blame her," I said.

"But just think, there never would have been me if she hadn't met my father. And what a loss to the world."

"You're so right," I agreed.

Then we both had a laughing fit, which is the way most of our conversations, however serious, end, especially at three in the morning.

My father went into the house to get his pipe and newspaper, and Tracy and I started to apply the paint remover.

"Is that your Human Relations paper sticking out of your pocket?" I asked.

"Uh huh. I said I'd bring it, didn't I? But you've got to swear you'll never tell anyone about it."

"Of course," I promised, wondering why she was so secretive. "I'll show you mine too. It's about E.J., and it's so innocent I don't care if Nelson reads it aloud in class."

"Well, I'd die if she read mine. You'll see why later."

"Once we get this gook on we have to wait at least twenty minutes till it dries. We'll go upstairs and swap stories then."

My father had come back outside, pulled his chair under a tree, and settled down with his paper. "You're doing a splendid job," he approved. "Don't forget the inside of the legs."

"Never fear," Tracy said, and slid on her back under the table, with the can of remover in one hand and the brush in the other.

"Almost done," I said, walking around the table.

Tracy, after a lot of moaning and groaning, finished the job on the legs and pulled herself up. "Care to inspect, J.?" she asked my father.

"I trust you guys implicitly. Just make sure you're back in thirty minutes for the hard part."

"Okay," I assured him. "We'll take a thirty-minute break."

"And when the job is finished, I'll fix the crew my special Western omelette. That's your reward for your services."

"Better than money any day," Tracy said.

"Tracy, you are so sensible," my father told her. Then he added, "Liz, you're a genius at picking friends."

"You know it!" I agreed.

As Tracy and I started into the house she mumbled to me, "You're so lucky."

I wasn't quite sure what she was talking about, but I was to find out very soon. Tracy, who I considered happy-go-lucky, was much more complicated than I ever imagined.

# 4

Tracy plopped down on the bed that had a few things on it. She picked up a lavender sweater and said, "This is great. I wish I could borrow it."

"You can."

"I could only fit in one shoulder."

"Don't be silly. You act as thought you're an Amazon."

"I am, compared to you."

"I can't help it if I'm what they call in the stores 'petite,'" I laughed. "Actually, Carolyn says you have the perfect figure for clothes. 'Tall and willowy' is the way she describes you."

"You're kidding! I never thought being five foot eight was an advantage." She sounded amazed.

"Why not?" I asked. "Everyone thinks I'm about twelve, instead of going on sixteen. No one believes that inside this tiny frame, I'm very sophisticated."

"You don't know what it's like to tower over every boy in the class. And being tall is really a drag in my gymnastics class. Even Tomo — he's our really cute Japanese instructor — admits it's a disadvantage. He's very diplomatic, but he once let it slip out that I have the most aptitude in the class, but my height gets in the way."

"That is a drag," I admitted, "but at least you look your age. I'll be thirty before anyone takes me for a grown-up."

"But you're so cute," Tracy said seriously.

"Thanks, but I'd rather be stunning." Then we both realized the absurdity of our conversation, and had a fit of giggles.

"Hey," I said abruptly, "we almost forgot to show our H.R. papers."

"Okay," Tracy said, slowly pulling it out of her jeans pocket. "But remember, you've got to promise not to tell anyone about it ever."

"You can trust me," I said as I took it from her. "It's really crinkled. You're not going to hand this in, are you?"

"I'll have to copy it over — that is, if I decide to hand it in at all. I have all day tomorrow to write something else. The truth is, I want you to read it and tell me if I sound crazy."

"You crazy? You're the most sane person I know."

"Don't be so sure."

I didn't know what she was getting at, but once I started reading her paper, I slowly began to realize that maybe Tracy covered up a lot of her feelings. Could it be that my best friend since fifth grade had dissembled all these years? Was her good-natured disposition just a front? One thing became clear, and that was that not having a father disturbed her much more than I ever imagined.

The title of her paper was "My Father*." It was only two pages long, but it revealed a great deal. Since I knew Tracy couldn't possibly remember her father, I thought she'd picked a weird subject to write about. Then I noticed the asterisk and saw at the bottom of the page, *A fantasy. The minute I started reading I could see that Tracy must daydream a lot about the kind of father she would like to have. She wrote:

> My father isn't handsome, but he has craggy good looks and is more than six feet two. He went to college on a football scholarship, but he was also a serious academic student. After seeing many injuries on the field during his freshman year, and suffering a broken bone himself, he developed a hate for football. But he felt obliged to continue playing in order to fulfill the requirements of his free tuition. His mother was widowed when he was eight years old. She earned money as a seamstress and was very ambitious for her only son. Thus, her values of hard work and drive were instilled in my father, who wanted to please her and live up to her expectations.
>
> Ironically, his exposure to pain inflicted by the contact sport of football triggered his

interest in orthopedics. Fortunately, he had an excellent scholastic record and earned another scholarship after graduation to a top medical school where he specialized in orthopedic surgery. As an intern at the Westchester Medical Center, he met my mother, who had just finished her nurse's training, and they were married less than a year later.

The paper went on to describe how her father is now one of the leading orthopedic surgeons in the country, but still has time to devote to his family. They always go to Maine the month of August and just last summer they rented a motor boat on the lake where the family rents a house, and her father taught her how to water-ski. Her final paragraph read:

> My father is a good example of someone whose personal values have been formed as a result of family tradition — in this case his mother's. Her attitudes and philosophy became his, and fortunately have been used for a force for good.

I was stunned after reading the paper and I couldn't think of anything to say. Also, I was a little embarrassed.

"Well?" Tracy said finally. "What about it?"

"It's very well written." I was hedging and I knew she wouldn't let me get away with that.

"That's not what I mean, Liz. I want to know if it's too ridiculous to hand in."

"Not if those are your feelings," I said thought-fully. "It'll show more imagination than anyone else's paper."

"Yeah, but am I making a fool of myself?"

"No, especially because you immediately say it's a fantasy. Besides, Nelson says she won't read any paper aloud that's marked confidential."

"I suppose you're right. I guess I'll just copy it over. Now, where's yours on E. J.?"

"Right here," I said, and pulled my paper out of my desk drawer. "It's dullsville, compared to yours."

"Let me be the judge of that."

Tracy began to read my paper and smiled to herself the whole time. When she finished, she burst out laughing.

"What's so funny?" I asked.

"It's not really funny," she explained. "It's just that you've captured her perfectly. I don't think I could ever be so objective about my mother."

"Maybe that's because you're more involved with your mother. I don't think it would be possible for me to describe my father accurately. I'm too close to him."

"Oh, oh. I can see us getting into one of our psychological raps."

Before I could continue, the focus of our discussion was calling upstairs. "Where are the troops?"

"Coming," I shouted. I stuffed the paper back in my desk drawer and then followed Tracy down the stairs.

My father had already removed the old paint

with a scraper. "When did you do all this, J.?" Tracy asked.

"You two were gone almost an hour. That gave me time to do step number two. Now it's ready for the fun part — sandpapering."

"Shrewdy," Tracy said. "What you really mean is the *hard* part."

"Well, certainly the most important. While you're doing that, I'll finish the crossword puzzle. Then I promise I'll fix that much-deserved omelette."

"I can't win with you," Tracy laughed.

I laughed, too, but I couldn't stop thinking about what Tracy had written. I wondered if everyone had a piece of one's self hidden under layers and layers of feelings — "innermosts" is how I thought of them.

I was going to find out an awful lot about my own "innermosts" before very long.

# 5 ————————

Tracy stayed until five o'clock. Then she had to leave in order to be home in time to have dinner with her mother, who was on the late shift at the hospital that night. Tracy always makes a point of not letting her mother be home alone at dinner even though I know sometimes it must be inconvenient. But she never has complained.

We planned to meet later at Jackie's house. There's sort of an unwritten rule that the four of us — me, Tracy, Ellen, and Jackie — get together Saturday night if we're free. Being "free" is a delicate way of saying we're not going out with anyone.

This Saturday will be one of the first in a long time that the four of us have been together. That's because Ellen, who is a young edition of Goldie Hawn, has just broken up with her boyfriend, Billy. Actually, he dumped her for Melissa, the class vamp. Melissa never talks much, she just lies back and smokes cigarettes out of a

long holder. We used to think she was the ulti-
mate in sophistication, but now we've decided
she has nothing to say, or to put it less politely,
she's stupid. However, there's no denying she
turns on the boys. I told Ellen that personally
I thought Billy would lose interest very soon because all Melissa is is a body with long black
hair. She might as well be a Cocker Spaniel. But
Ellen refuses to talk about it. She keeps up a
brave front, but I know she's been hurt and is
really grateful to have something to do Saturday
night.

My love life is non-existent. Carolyn says it's
not normal, but I've tried to explain that I'd
rather be with my girlfriends than go out with
some nerd. David is always asking me out, but
he's so serious I think he may be fearful of breaking his face if he smiles. Carolyn admits she
would rather die than not go out with a boy on
Saturday night.

Just the other night we had a discussion about
this very subject when we were doing the dishes.
My parents had gone into New York to visit
friends for dinner, and Carolyn and I were on
our own. Actually, Carolyn and I don't really
fight like a lot of sisters, but we don't agree on
anything.

I was rinsing and she was putting them in the
dishwasher. I think she prefers that because she's
afraid of ruining her nails.

In the middle of doing the dishes the phone
rang. It was David, who asked me to go to the
movies Saturday night. I explained that I had

other plans and would call him later because my hands were soapy. I figured that would give me time to think up a legitimate excuse not to go out with him. It's not that I don't like him. It's just that he's boring.

When I hung up, Carolyn said, "I don't believe you. You really would rather be with the girls."

"Of course. They're much more fun."

"Well, I think you're unreal."

"I won't settle for creeps," I said defensively.

"Are you suggesting I do?" she asked haughtily.

"What about Larry?" Larry is the good-natured roly-poly in the senior class. He's always had a crush on Carolyn but she only goes out with him in case of emergency — that is, when for some reason one of the really cute guys has stood her up.

"The last time I went out with Larry was for the last baseball game of the school year. If you remember correctly, I was supposed to go with Tom, but he unexpectedly went away for the weekend with his family."

"So why not go with Nancy or Sara?" They were Carolyn's closest friends.

"They're not boys!" Carolyn explained.

"They're persons!" I insisted.

"You just don't understand," she said, shaking her head in despair.

I was thinking about this conversation as I helped my father clean up the mess from the table. Here it was Saturday, and I was perfectly happy at the prospect of spending the evening with my friends who didn't happen to be boys. Since Jackie, Ellen, and Tracy feel the same way I do, I figure I can't be too crazy. Just because Carolyn is older doesn't mean she's right about everything!

Tracy had already left when E.J. and Carolyn came home. My mother pulled the car into the driveway, and the minute she stepped out she spotted the table. We had stained it a deep brown and it had a rich grain finish.

"That table is beautiful," my mother told us as she walked around it, inspecting it carefully. Then she reached up to plant a kiss on my father's cheek. His hands were filled with newspapers, and he looked very pleased.

"Not bad," Carolyn said admiringly.

"Maybe we should go in business," my father said, and gave me a slow wink.

"Hey, Elizabeth, come upstairs and I'll show you our purchases," Carolyn said, dragging a bundle out of the car. "We got you the cutest T-shirt."

"Sure," I said, and followed her into the house and upstairs into her bedroom. Her room looks more like a sitting room. It's all done in pink and white and has a daybed covered in solid pink with checkered pillow shams. For her sixteenth birthday my parents gave her a dressing table with a mirror surrounded by light bulbs — the kind that movies stars use.

She was given a choice, within financial limits of course, of what she wanted, and E.J. thought it was a wonderful idea. My father went along with it, but I could tell he didn't entirely approve. "Are you sure?" he asked her.

"Absolutely," she answered.

"Every Southern girl had a vanity table when I was growing up," E.J. drawled. Whenever she mentions the South, E.J.'s accent gets even thicker.

"Okay," my father said reluctantly. "You only have one sixteenth birthday."

Her friends, Nancy and Sara, gave Carolyn a magnifying mirror that sits on top of the dressing table. I'm always irresistibly drawn to that table when I'm in Carolyn's room, and I can't help gazing in that mirror which magnifies every defect to an alarming degree.

Carolyn has zillions of cosmetics. Last summer she worked as a mother's helper for a month at Cape Cod. She admitted to me that she hated the job that required taking care of a bratty four-year-old, but that she wanted to pick up some extra change that would keep her in cosmetics for a while. She loves trying on new faces and always suggests that I wear lip gloss at least. But I'm just not interested. Still, I can't stop staring at myself in that mirror, which is exactly what I was doing when Carolyn was opening packages.

"If you can tear yourself away for a minute, look at this," she said. "This is for you."

She tossed over a navy-blue T-shirt that had a tiny red heart on the sleeve.

"Hey, this is cute," I said, holding the T-shirt against me and swiveling around so I could admire myself in the mirror.

"I got one too," she said.

"You did?" I was amazed. "Ever since you were ten years old you've insisted on not wearing the same things I do."

"That's because I wanted to be grown up, dummy. Now that I am, it doesn't matter."

"I get it."

"Actually, mother found this for you, but I couldn't resist it. It'll be a great conversation piece. No one can wear that and not have at least ten guys say something about wearing your heart on your sleeve."

"You think of everything," I laughed. "What else did you get?"

"This!" she exclaimed, and whirled around, holding a black dirndl skirt with tiny, bright red flowers to her waist. "It'll look smashing with my red Danskin top, don't you think?"

"Terrific," I agreed. "Sexy, too."

"You're learning," she said. "I'll even let you borrow it sometime."

"You know you're safe."

"Don't be so sure. You're the type that may become an overnight full-fledged femme fatale."

"First I better learn how to use eye shadow."

"Why don't you practice right now?"

"I'm not ready yet."

"You're hopeless. Anyhow, I haven't got time to argue because I'm being picked up at six-thirty and I'm nowhere near ready."

"Who is it tonight?" I asked.

"Tonight it's Jesse. His cousin is in town and a bunch of us are going to the new disco that opened in White Plains."

"Have fun. I have to go now, too. We're meeting at Jackie's and going to the pizza parlor."

"Have a good time. And really, if you want a lesson in makeup I have some free time tomorrow between ten and eleven."

"Thanks," I said. "Not tomorrow, but you'll be the first to know when."

As I left the room and closed the door behind me, I couldn't help thinking that as sisters go, she's really not so bad.

# 6

Tracy was already at Jackie's house when I arrived. In fact, she answered the door. I figured Jackie's parents, Mr. and Mrs. Johnson, must be out, otherwise Mrs. Johnson would be bustling around, asking questions. I think their family roles must be reversed, because Jackie is so sensible and her mother is a scatterbrain. Jackie has straight black hair and wears wire-framed glasses that make her look very sedate even though she's really pretty. Sometimes I wonder if she isn't hiding behind her glasses.

Mrs. Johnson, on the other hand, tries to act like one of us. She uses expressions like "cool" and "far out," but always in the wrong places. I have a rough time not laughing at her. Once I was telling about a Woody Allen movie that I loved and Mrs. Johnson said, "It must have been off the wall." I looked at Tracy and we both cracked up, but Jackie just groaned. The one good thing about Jackie's mother is that she doesn't seem to notice our reactions and just keeps right on babbling.

"How did you make it so early?" I asked Tracy as I followed her into the foyer.

"My mother actually had a 'date' for dinner before she went on her shift," she answered gleefully. "She apologized for not having dinner with me. Isn't that crazy? I've been hoping all along that she'd go out with someone."

"That's terrific. Maybe your paper won't be such a fantasy after all."

"Ssshhh," Tracy whispered. "You promised not to breathe a word."

"Nobody's listening," I said softly. "Where are they?"

"You know Jackie's parents are out or you'd see her mother. And Jackie's in the kitchen getting some junk food that's guaranteed to put bumps on our skin and holes in our teeth — in preparation for the pizza that we'll have later. And Ellen isn't here yet."

Just then Jackie burst through the kitchen door that led to the dining room off the hall. She was carrying a tray with glasses and Cokes and a huge bowl of potato chips. "Hiya," Jackie said. "Let's go into the den. I promised not to mess up the living room."

"Hi," I said. "You mean we're allowed in the 'heart of the house'?" That's how Mrs. Johnson describes the den. She says it's her favorite room, and it does have everything. The walls are lined with books, there's a stereo set, and smack in the middle is a bridge table with four chairs. It's a perfect room for four people, providing they sit down at the table.

Jackie has explained to me that her parents are avid game players — everything from chess and Scrabble to bridge and gin rummy, and that's why they have a permanent table. "We call it the Truth Table. That's because last year the four of us used to have "Truth Time" sessions around it. We'd pick a subject like "What would you like to change most about yourself?" or "What do you like least about your parents?" It was fascinating to be able to find out certain truths about yourself and about the others, but dredging up the innermosts and exposing them hurts, and half the time one of us would wind up in tears. We finally decided that "Truth Time" was immature, but what we really meant was too painful. We still talk about a lot of personal things, but not in a compulsory manner. Now we bend over backwards to avoid sensitive subjects.

We were seated at the table, digging into the potato-chip bowl while Jackie handed us our glasses of Coke.

"Remember," Jackie warned, "when Ellen comes, let's not bring up the subject of Billy and Melissa."

"Course not," Tracy agreed.

"No problem," I said, just as the doorbell rang.

While she was gone, Tracy suddenly looked wistful. "Sometimes I wish I had love problems."

"Don't worry, you will," I assured her, "but we can't talk about that now."

"I know."

Then Jackie and Ellen came back into the room, and sank into the chairs. Ellen didn't even bother to say hello. She plunged right in, talking about what was on all our minds. "I still don't see what he sees in her," she said belligerently.

There was an awkward silence, because this was the first time Ellen had volunteered any information about how she felt. Ellen looked at each one of us, but we kept this idiotic silence.

"Say something!" she insisted. "Why are you acting like the sphinx?"

"We thought you didn't want to talk about it," I said finally.

"I didn't, that's true," she said sheepishly. "But then I decided it's all I can think about, and you're my friends. My parents sure don't understand. My father keeps talking about puppy love, and my mother says she'll buy me the pair of Frye boots that I've wanted for the past year, hoping that will make me feel better. That's how much she knows!"

"I can't understand why parents don't think we suffer," Jackie said. "Probably they can't remember how they felt at fifteen."

"Or maybe they don't want to remember, and have covered up with a lot of defenses," I suggested.

"That's what my mother says," Tracy added. "She says feelings are stronger when you're young. Then you learn to protect yourself."

"Well, I've decided it's better to let it all hang out. I mean what good does it do to pretend something's not happening, if it's happening."

"You're right, Ellen. I really admire your honesty. Sometimes I think if I pretend something that's bothering me isn't, it will go away," I admitted.

"Me, too," said Jackie.

"Like what?" Ellen asked.

"Like I can't talk about it, because that's admitting it's happening."

Then we started laughing because we could see the conversation was going in circles. Ellen said suddenly, "This is the first time I've even smiled in days. To tell you the truth, I didn't think I'd ever recover. Now I think there's hope."

"And I know you won't believe this, but I wish I had something to recover from," Tracy volunteered.

"You mean, you wish you were in love?" Jackie asked.

"Exactly."

"It's not worth it," Ellen groaned.

"I wouldn't mind trying it," I said.

"Me neither," Jackie said.

"I can't believe what's happening," Ellen said. "I came here in the depths of despair, feeling really sorry for myself, and I wind up feeling sorry for you. Did you guys plan it this way?"

"Don't be ridiculous," Jackie told her.

"Better to have loved and lost than never to have loved at all," Tracy offered, seriously. Then she asked, "Who said that?"

"Probably one of the Romantic poets," Ellen said.

"Nope," Jackie piped up. "It's a Victorian poet. Tennyson, to be exact."

No one questioned her because Jackie is inevitably right. She pretends not to study that much, but I think she's a closet intellectual. She has stacks of books in her room and she gets all A's, but she never talks about it.

"Whoever said it, it's a beautiful thought," Tracy said dreamily.

"If you like that sort of thing," Ellen growled.

"Well, I do like that sort of thing. Just because you've had an unhappy love affair doesn't mean that we shouldn't consider the possibility," Tracy snapped.

Ellen was taken aback and didn't say anything. And for the second time today Tracy had surprised me. "Take it easy, Trace," I said. "We're just talking."

"What is it with you?" Jackie asked her gently.

"I don't know," Tracy said, looking bewildered. For a minute, I thought she might burst into tears. Then she quickly recovered and said, "Maybe I'm Dr. Jekyll and Mr. Hyde . . . only female."

That made us all laugh and I was so relieved that I blurted out, "Thank goodness for your sense of humor."

Jackie said, "We've managed to polish off the potato chips. And in order to avoid any more heavy discussions, I think we should get away from the Truth Table. I think no matter how hard we try, this table sends out rays of pain and anguish."

"Personally, I think it's pizza time," I said.

"Me, too," said Tracy. "And once we're out of the house, we can figure out our strategy against it." She pointed her finger at the table.

# 7

I think that life has cycles, something like a roller coaster. Everything will be going along smoothly and suddenly there'll be a change, sometimes just a bumpy stretch, and other times a gigantic upheaval. The only thing to do is hang in and hope that things will even out again.

On the way home from the pizza parlor, after saying goodnight to the others, Ellen and I walked off together because we live only two blocks apart. I told her my roller coaster theory. She agreed, but said right now she'd prefer a Ferris wheel where the ride is considerably smoother.

The following week Ms. Nelson spent a whole class period talking about how relationships change, often due to external circumstances, but always because the ingredients are there for change. She said that often hostility is buried, but will surface when someone becomes angry no matter how hard that person tries to hide it. Then she asked us to write a paper describing a changing relationship.

It was an interesting assignment but for the moment I couldn't think of what to write about. I guess I must have frowned or groaned or something because Ms. Nelson noticed me and smiled. "Don't worry if you can't think of anything right away," she advised. "The paper isn't due for ten days, and I guarantee if you keep your eyes open, you'll come up with something."

I wasn't so sure. In keeping with my roller coaster ride, I thought I was on a smooth stretch . . . no major disagreements with E.J.; as always I was getting along with my father; Carolyn and I were giving each other enough space; and my friends were my friends.

Little did I know how right Ms. Nelson was, for in less than ten days I had the perfect subject, one I would have preferred to live without. The "incident" happened the Friday before the paper was due, and the only good thing about it was that finally I had a subject to write about.

It all started because I had a baby-sitting job, something I don't exactly love, but it's a good way to pick up some change. I get an allowance that's adequate, but it doesn't allow any real extravagances, such as a new Head tennis racquet, which costs a fortune, and I don't really need. In fact, my parents gave me a beautiful wooden racquet for Christmas and it's still good as new.

Jackie and I are doubles partners on the tennis team at school, and one day she let me try out her racquet. Maybe it was coincidence but I'd never played so well, and after that day I was determined to earn enough money baby-sitting to buy myself a Head.

Jane and Jim Gardner live around the corner from us and they have a two-year-old girl. E.J. refers to the Gardners as that adorable young couple. I personally don't think they're so young — Jane is at least twenty-five — but they are very nice and they always tell me how their kid, Miriam, likes me better than any other sitter.

On Friday, the Gardners had asked me to come over at seven, help put Miriam to bed, and plan to stay until about eleven because they were going out to dinner and the movies with another couple. That same evening E.J. and John were going to the theater in New York and planned to be home about the same time I was. And Carolyn was going out with Steve. Steve is practically a legend in our school and every girl sooner or later falls in love with him. He's always been really cool about women, but Carolyn has been determined to change that and I think she's succeeding.

Before I left to go to the Gardner's I went into my mother's room to tell her when I would be leaving. She was finishing dressing and Carolyn, draped in a towel, was asking if she could borrow some French perfume.

"Where you going?" I asked.

"Nancy's having some kids over for a barbecue and I'm going with Steve."

"Not something you need French perfume for exactly," I couldn't help saying.

"You wouldn't understand," she said.

"Now girls," E.J. admonished. "Let's not fight."

"She started it," Carolyn pointed out. In a way she was right, and I guess the idea of baby-sitting while she was at a barbecue didn't put me in the greatest of moods. Before I could defend myself Carolyn turned to my mother and held up a tiny bottle. "Can I borrow this?"

"Go ahead, honey. But save some for the next time. Incidentally, what time are you leaving?"

"Steve's picking me up at about seven."

"And you, Elizabeth?"

"I'm leaving in a few minutes. Supposed to be at the Gardner's at seven."

"Have a good time, girls. I have to run right now. Your father's already got the car out."

"See ya," I said, as she grabbed her bag and hurried out of the room.

"Enjoy the play," Carolyn called after her. "And thanks for the perfume."

After she was gone, Carolyn stood before the mirror over the dresser and carefully dabbed perfume behind her ears.

"What time are you coming home?" she asked casually.

"Probably about eleven. The Gardners are going to dinner and a movie."

"Well, I probably won't see you till tomorrow."

"See ya," I said, and left her dabbing on the inside of her wrists.

## 8

When I got to the Gardner's, Miriam ran up to me and grabbed me around the legs. I picked her up and gave her a hug. I don't consider myself very maternal, but I guess a lot of reactions are instinctive.

"See," Jane remarked, "she really loves you. But now she's so excited you'll have to read her a story before she goes to sleep."

Then Jim came down the stairs. "Hello, Liz," he said. "I can see Miriam's got her favorite person."

"Hi," I said, thinking this isn't exactly a barbecue, but the Gardners are good for my ego.

"Help yourself to any soda that's in the fridge, and there are some freshly made sugar cookies in the cookie jar," Jane offered.

"Thanks," I said.

"I'll call you before we go to the movies, probably around eight-thirty, just to make sure everything's okay."

"Don't worry, Miriam will take good care of me."

"It's reassuring to know you're in good hands," Jim said, helping Jane with her coat, and laughing.

After they left I tucked Miriam in bed and read her a story, which she couldn't possibly understand, about a dog who befriends a cat. Before I was finished reading, she was sound asleep. Then I went downstairs, helped myself to a Coke and cookies, and went into the living room to watch television. I tuned in on an old Hitchcock movie and before I knew it it was eight-thirty. Jane had said she would call then, and since she is very conscientious about Miriam, I was surprised that the phone didn't ring just as the commercial started. When another fifteen minutes passed, I figured she was just having too good a time and forgot.

At nine o'clock I went upstairs to make sure Miriam was all right. She was fast asleep and as I went downstairs I was startled to hear someone at the door. All sorts of horror stories flashed through my head, and then I heard Jim's voice. "Don't be frightened, Liz. It's just us — home early."

"What happened?" I asked.

"Our friend Sue got sick in the restaurant and had to go home. We went to Sue and Rob's house for a while, and then decided it was too late for the movie, so we came home."

"This is the third time Sue's pulled some act like this. I think she does it on purpose," Jane growled.

"You're being silly," Jim said. "Last time she wanted to make it a short evening because she wanted to visit her father who had just come home from the hospital. And tonight I think it was the MSG they put in the Chinese food. I don't think we should keep going back to the Shanghai Garden."

"You're always defending Sue."

"You're crazy. I'm just trying to find an explanation."

"Well, I think it's psychological. You know she's got a thing about you and she's guilty about it. Every time she's with you and Rob, she throws up."

"Jane, darling, are you serious?"

"Deadly."

"Now I know you're crazy. Rob is one of my oldest friends. No matter who he married, he would still be my friend. It's just a lucky break that we all like Sue."

"Speak for youself."

Meanwhile, I was getting more and more embarrassed, wishing I was anywhere but on the bottom step, with no escape. When there was finally a pause in the conversation, I said quickly, "I better be going. Miriam was fine and the cookies were delicious."

"Good," Jane snapped, and brushed past me upstairs.

Jim looked at me and shrugged his shoulders. Then he stuck his hand in his pocket and pulled out a ten-dollar bill, which he handed to me.

"This is too much," I protested, "and I don't have any change."

"It's not too much. Ordinarily we'd be home much later, and you would have earned it."

"Thanks a lot. I really appreciate it." Then I added, "I hope everything is okay."

"It will be. Jane just gets ticked off when things don't go according to schedule, and she really did want to see the new Alan Alda movie."

"Call me next time you need a sitter," I said, as I went into the living room to pick up my bag and sweater.

"You're number one on our list," Jim said as he held the door open for me. "Get home safely."

"See ya," I said, "and thanks again."

All the way home I kept thinking about the Gardners — "that adorable young couple." They look like the All-American family. Jane actually was a model for *Seventeen* when she was in high school. She still looks like a teenager — trim and dark-haired, with perfect white skin. Jim is the perfect counterpart. He had been a three-letter man in college and now worked in advertising. He's always good-natured but I sometimes wonder about Jane. She's obviously not as sweet as she pretends. I thought maybe they'd be a good couple to write about for my Changing Relationship paper, but then I really didn't know that much about them. Maybe I could make some things up. I only had two days left.

When I got to my house, only the light over the entrance was lit, and one lamp in my parents' bedroom. They always leave that one on so that the house doesn't look empty.

I knew no one would be home and I let myself in with the key. I flicked the light switch in the hall, and at the same time I sensed that someone was in the darkened living room. I had a moment of panic. "Who's there?" I asked, trying to keep in control.

I heard some frantic rustling sounds. Then I heard Carolyn's voice.

"You're not supposed to be here," she said shrilly.

"Neither are you."

"You could at least knock."

"Why should I? No one was home — I thought."

Steve switched on the light next to the couch and I noticed his hair was rumpled, and Carolyn looked slightly disheveled.

"Hi," Steve said, smiling. "I guess it's true about kid sisters. If I give you a quarter will you go away?"

I couldn't help laughing. "Seeing as I just earned a lot of quarters, you can't buy me off."

"Hey, Carolyn, you didn't tell me what a cute sister you had."

"Her?" Carolyn said, raising her eyebrows and looking at me. She acted as though there might have been someone else in the room who Steve was referring to.

"What are you doing here?" I said innocently.

"Don't ask," Steve said.

"It's none of your business," Carolyn barked. "What are *you* doing here?"

"I live here," I answered sarcastically.

"That's not what I mean. I distinctly remember you saying you wouldn't be home till eleven. It's not even ten yet."

"And I distinctly remember you saying you were going to a barbecue at Nancy's."

"Our plans changed."

"Obviously."

"If you tell E.J. I'll kill you."

"I thought you told her everything."

"This is not the time to discuss it."

"Listen, I'm not going to say anything. Stop worrying."

"Thanks," she said, sounding very relieved.

Meanwhile Steve had been watching us silently. Finally he said, "You two are great. All I've got is a kid brother who keeps hassling me to play ball. I can see it's much more interesting to have a kid sister."

I couldn't tell if he was paying me a compliment or trying to make the situation less awkward. Anyhow, I felt like a fool standing there so I told them I was going upstairs to write a paper for my Human Relations class. "It was due Monday, and I haven't even started."

"What's it on?" Carolyn asked, trying to be friendly.

"You," I answered, backing out of the room and leaving her looking completely bewildered.

"Me?" she said.

"Don't worry, I'm just going to tell it like it is."

It was hard to believe that Ms. Nelson was absolutely right — in less than ten days I had a subject to write about. I did elaborate somewhat, but basically I kept to what I saw as the facts. The main point was that Carolyn appeared to be the perfect daughter, confiding in her mother about everything, but actually having a private life that she wouldn't discuss. E.J. would have been shocked if she had discovered that Carolyn had ever lied to her. I added a few psychological explanations about how Carolyn had a need for approval and therefore pretended to do exactly what E.J. wanted her to do.

Carolyn seemed so poised and confident to me. Now I wondered if she didn't have a lot of insecurities, and her sophistication was just a cover-up.

I was sitting at my desk when there was a knock at my door.

"Come in," I said. It was Carolyn, who had pulled herself together and was no longer flustered.

"Listen, we really are going to the pizza parlor now. You promise you won't tell mother that I didn't go to Nancy's?"

"I promise."

"And what about that paper you're writing? I don't exactly enjoy being used as a specimen."

"Don't worry. The papers are confidential."

"Will you show it to me at least?"

"Nope."

"Why not?"

"Because it's my paper. I shouldn't even have told you about it."

"Well, if that's how you want to be." She gave me her raised eyebrow look and shrugged her shoulders as if she couldn't care less.

I knew that she was dying to see what I would write, but had to retain her cool image. It was part of her act. She didn't know it but she was providing me with even more material.

After she left, I thought a lot about "appearances," and wondered whether everyone put on a "party" face. Lately, it seemed, I was seeing everyone close to me in a new light; Tracy had fantasies about having a father; the Gardners weren't Mr. and Mrs. Perfect; and now Carolyn seemed less than the ideal daughter.

I wondered if everyone, including me, kept their real feelings under wraps until something *real* happened that made them reveal themselves. So far, I had to admit, I'd tried to go along with what was expected of me.

# 9_____

One of E.J.'s Southern hang-ups is that her daughters must take up something musical. She wants us to be well-rounded and claims such an interest might lead to a hobby we can enjoy all our lives. I didn't give her an argument, and I think she was delighted when I was in eighth grade and told her I wanted to take ballet. Ballet is what she took as a young girl, and she is convinced that it makes one graceful. "Not that I do it anymore," she explained, "but everyone tells me how well I move, and I know that's because of my ballet lessons."

Carolyn is taking the flute. She once confided to me that she didn't love the instrument that much, but it was the lightest one to carry. She said she wasn't about to break her back carrying a cello around, even though she liked the sound. Her friend Sara plays the double bass and Carolyn always teases her about getting a hernia.

My ballet class meets every Wednesday, and Annabella is the same teacher I've had for three years. She's not that old, but she has an old-fashioned attitude about teaching. She is very strict about working at the bar, and practicing our positions. It seems we have very little time to actually dance. It's only the last twenty minutes that she puts on a record and lets us fly, and then it's totally disorganized. To tell the truth I've been getting a little bored with ballet — not that I don't like it, but I've mastered all the basic stuff and Annabella isn't challenging us with anything new.

I'd like to find a way out, but what and how are the questions. The year had already started, I didn't want to insult Annabella by dropping out before the semester had ended, and E.J. would have a fit. It wasn't worth it, so I might as well suffer in silence.

I had no idea that a series of coincidences would get me out of ballet, and actually change my whole life. Well, maybe it wasn't coincidence. My history teacher, Mr. Ramrod — who has the world's most unsuitable name because he's short, bespectacled, and hunched over — has a framed quote on his desk that says: "Coincidence, if traced far enough back, becomes inevitable" — *Inscription on a Hindu temple.*

He uses this theme in all his teaching, maintaining that there are certain impulses in history that force things to happen, and although they may appear to come about coincidentally, there is an overall scheme.

It started the Wednesday before the long Thanksgiving weekend. Tracy and I had walked over to the Y together and went directly to the locker room. The one lucky thing was that Tracy's gymnastics class was the same time as my ballet and we could walk back and forth together. I finished changing into my leotard first and slumped down on the bench to wait for Tracy. I guess I must have been looking glum because Tracy said, "What's the matter?"

"Nothing, really," I answered. "Just boring ballet."

"Why don't you switch to gymnastics? I think you'd love it."

"Too complicated. Annabella would be insulted, I don't know if I could get into Tomo's class, and besides, E.J. would have a heart attack."

"In that case . . ." Tracy didn't finish her sentence but tied her hair back with a rubber band and said, "Let's go."

We went into the corridor and I waved to Tracy as she entered the gymnasium, which is exactly opposite my ballet classroom. "Have fun," I said.

"You, too. I'll meet you in the locker room."

I strolled into the ballet room and exchanged greetings with the ten or twelve kids who were already there, most of them leaning against the bar which stretches across one end of the room. Then Annabella appeared.

"Hello, people," she said briskly. She wore a black leotard and except for her muscular legs looked exactly like a young boy, even though she's at least thirty years old. Her dark hair is closely cropped, but she wears a slash of bright red lipsick on her lips, as though to make sure no one mistakes her for a man. She's not a bad egg but her super-efficiency turns me off.

"People," she said, "I must tell you that class will be dismissed thirty-five minutes early today. It being the Thanksgiving weekend, I'm going upstate to be with my family, and I must catch the five-thirty bus. Now let's work very hard to make up for the time you'll be missing. Positions, now!" She clapped her hands three times and we lined up at the bar.

I went through the movements automatically, my mind on a million other things. Before I knew it the time was up, and Annabella was hurrying off, saying, "People, have a lovely weekend, and don't forget to practice."

"Happy turkey," somebody screeched, and then everyone took up the cry, "Happy turkey, happy turkey." There was a lot of milling around and chattering, and I slipped out of the room and wandered across the hall to the gym.

I slid down on the floor near the entrance, as unobtrusively as possible. There were nine girls of all ages, all ready to do their thing. Some were taking turns doing rolls on the floor exercise mat. A couple were lined up waiting to practice on the balance beam, which was on the floor, so that if they fell they wouldn't have far to go. The others were standing in line, waiting to vault. Tomo was standing by the vault, helping each girl leap over. None of them were too advanced, and as I was watching, one little kid about ten stopped cold when she got to the vault and Tomo practically had to lift her over.

The whole thing looked like a lot of fun.

Tracy, who was waiting in line, spotted me almost as soon as I came in. "Hi, Liz," she called, and waved.

I waved back. Tomo glanced at me and Tracy said, "That's my best friend, Liz, even though she takes ballet."

"Want to join us?" Tomo asked.

"I've never done it," I answered.

"All the more reason. Are you warmed up from your ballet class?"

"Too warm."

"Good. We're going to work out on the bars. Watch how it's done, and then you can try it."

"I'd love to," I said, standing up.

"Okay, everybody, line up for the bars. Liz, you stand by me so you can see better."

I walked over to the spot he was pointing to, and felt a rush of excitement at the prospect of trying something new.

"Everyone, don't forget to chalk your hands." I noticed a box of chalk on the floor beside the bars. Tomo picked up a chalk bag and passed it to the first person in line. When she was finished with it he handed it to me. "That's to reduce the friction on the bars," he explained. Then he turned to the others. "We'll work the Cast first. Keep your bodies firm, your feet together, and make the movement smooth."

I watched carefully as each girl grasped the bar, rested the front of her hips against it, and then swung her legs forward and back so that her body stretched out behind her. I couldn't wait to try it myself.

When each girl had finished her turn, Tomo said to me, "Ready?"

"Sure," I said. I grasped the bar and imitated the others. It was easier than I thought it would be.

"That's good," Tomo said. "Now we'll do a Back Hip Circle. That incorporates the Cast, plus a circle backward around the bar. Tracy, you demonstrate."

Tracy came to the head of the line and poised herself at the bar. Then she executed the move, perfectly, I thought. I was surprised to hear Tomo say, "That was a little sloppy. Remember, keep your knees together."

"I can't think of everything," Tracy grumbled, and went to the end of the line.

When the others had taken their turn, with varying degrees of success, Tomo turned to me. "Do you dare?"

"Can't wait," I said eagerly.

"Don't rush," he advised as I hurriedly grasped the bar. "Take a deep breath before you begin."

I breathed deeply, then grasped the bar, swung forward and back, and when my body came back to the bar, made a full circle.

"That was excellent," Tomo complimented me. "Stay after class a few minutes. I'd like to talk to you."

"Okay," I said, curious about what he wanted to say.

Tomo then announced to the others who were lined up, ready to perform again, "Sorry, everyone. It's time to go now."

There was a lot of groaning and moaning and one girl coaxed, "Just one more time?"

"Come on," Tomo teased, "I'm sure you're all anxious to get home and help in the kitchen. Have a wonderful holiday!"

There were shouts of "Happy Thanksgiving," and "Bye, Tomo," and "See ya next week." It was obvious that everyone liked Tomo and wanted to please him.

Tracy and I were the only ones left. Tomo said to Tracy, "I wanted to see your friend here do some floor work. Trace, you show her how to do a bridge."

"I'd be happy to," Tracy said, and promptly stretched out on her back, her hands above her shoulders, and made an arc with her body.

"Perfect," Tomo praised her. "Now you try it, Liz."

I copied Tracy and arched my back as much as I could. "Hold it," Tomo said, "to the count of five." Then he counted slowly to five and said, "Relax."

"You're good," Tracy exclaimed. "It took me weeks to do that."

"Can you do splits on both sides? Show her how, Tracy."

Tracy gracefully stretched out her long legs, doing a split first on one side and then on the other.

"Beautiful," I said.

"Now you try it," Tomo urged.

I guess because of my ballet exercises I could do the split easily. Tracy clapped her hands as I held the position.

"Can you do a Chinese split?" Tomo asked.

"What's that?"

"I'll show you," Tracy volunteered and promptly stretched one leg out to the right and one to the left.

"That's good, Tracy," Tomo said.

"I'll try it," I said, and to my surprise managed to perform the Chinese split easily.

"Hold it," Tomo ordered, and again counted to five.

"That really pulls," I remarked.

"It's supposed to," Tracy explained.

"I can't believe you haven't practiced this before." Tomo looked genuinely surprised.

"Well, we do a lot of exercises in ballet."

"You have a strong body and are unusually supple. You're a natural for gymnastics."

"You mean it?"

"I know you'd love it," Tracy added.

"Is there room in the class?"

"We have room for exactly one more. In fact, you'd be a perfect replacement for Geraldine. She had good potential, but her family had to move to the Midwest one month after school started. We're down to nine in the class, but I can handle ten."

"I really would like to join."

"Well, think it over. No pressure, but I honestly believe you're a natural, and Tracy knows I always tell it like it is."

"You're not kidding," Tracy said, laughing. "Sometime we *kill* ourselves for Tomo, and all he says is, 'still a little sloppy.'"

"You wouldn't want me to lie," Tomo said innocently.

"Maybe just a little," Tracy suggested.

"Now, you better get going. It's getting late and I don't want to be accused of being a slave driver."

"Which he is," Tracy said to me, covering her mouth as though she were whispering.

"Don't believe her, Liz. But try and find out for yourself. I'll fix things up with Annabella, if that's the problem."

"There's one other problem, but I'll try."

"I'll work on her," Tracy said. "And I'll see you next week."

"Thanks for everything," I said. "I hope to see you next week, too."

"You can, you know," Tomo said. "So long for now."

"Bye," I said, feeling heady and confused. One thing I knew for sure — a door had been opened and I would have to find out where it led.

## *10*_____

On the way home Tracy said, "I knew you'd love gymnastics. And isn't Tomo great? I think every girl in the class has a crush on him."

"I can see why," I admitted. "And I can tell you're one of his favorites."

"I don't know about that," Tracy said modestly, "but he did tell me last week that I should definitely prepare for the local gymnastics meet."

"Terrific. What happens after that?"

"There are a lot of contests, and you keep advancing by doing well. In other words, if I score well in the local meet in December, I will qualify for the regional contest in the spring."

"You'll be famous yet," I kidded her.

"What about you? At least you should start the class."

"I'd love it, but you know E.J. She'll never want me to quit ballet, and I think she has some Neanderthal idea that gymnastics isn't feminine."

"What about your father? I bet John would think it's a good idea."

"Probably. I'll have to try the idea out on them tonight."

We'd arrived at Tracy's street and I still had a few blocks to go. "No matter what happens, I really enjoyed today," I told her. "Thanks for asking me to join."

"I just hope you can come next week. It'll be so much fun."

"I hope so, too."

"Let me know what happens. You can always use me as an example of femininity in your argument with E.J. I mean, I'm not exactly built like a boy!"

"Hardly," I agreed. We both were laughing as we waved good-bye.

I quickly sobered up, though, when I thought of E.J.'s reaction to my wanting to take gymnastics. Maybe, I thought hopefully, she wouldn't be as opposed to the idea as I anticipated. I guess I've never quite recovered from her thinking of me as a tomboy. I don't really like that image anymore, although it didn't bother me so much when I was a little kid. In her mind, I'm sure, it's permanently engraved.

When I arrived at the house, E.J. was bustling around the kitchen, my father was opening a bottle of wine, and Carolyn was finishing setting the table.

"Where were you, Elizabeth?" E.J. asked. "You never get home this late after ballet."

"Ballet let out early and I went to watch gymnastics."

"And gymnastics gets out after six-thirty?"

"Not exactly. I sort of tried out for it." I tried to sound casual.

E.J. was carrying a large casserole filled with chicken and dumplings, and a variety of vegetables that smelled delicious all the way into the dining room. "You what?" she shrieked. "Quick, John, get out a trivet before I drop this."

My father took a brass trivet out of the buffet and neatly slid it toward my mother's end of the table.

"Now, what's this all about?" my mother asked. I had just finished washing my hands at the kitchen sink and strolled into the dining room, where my mother had already begun to dish out the casserole.

"Obviously she's going to take gymnastics," Carolyn observed as she pulled up her chair.

"Who said?" E.J. was spooning out the gravy so briskly I was surprised it stayed on the plate. I could tell she was having difficulty keeping cool.

"It's a lot of fun," I said. "And I'm really bored with ballet."

"Fun? It seems to me that gymnastics is meant for everyone who can't dance, or do any other sport well, for that matter. It's just a form of extended exercise that'll probably make you musclebound."

"That's not true, Mother. Haven't you ever seen the exhibitions on television?"

"Not if I can help it."

"It's a beautiful sport."

"Beauty is in the eye of the beholder. I think it looks like a contortionist's idea of heaven."

Even I had to laugh at that, but I knew that E.J. wasn't kidding about being turned off by the sport. I was waiting for my father to say something. I consider him the voice of reason, and I knew if he agreed with E.J., my entertaining the idea of switching to gymnastics was a lost cause.

"How did you even happen to try out?" he asked.

I repeated the story about ballet getting out early, and watching the gymnastics class, and Tomo asking me to join in. "I did a few exercises and Tomo told me I was a natural."

"It's not a very social sport," Carolyn commented.

"You mean I won't meet any boys?" I couldn't help sounding slightly disgusted. "That doesn't happen to be the chief aim of my existence."

"You don't know what you're missing."

"Maybe *you* don't." I wasn't sure what I meant by that, but I was really getting mad.

"That's not the point," my father intervened.

"What is the point?" E.J. asked.

"The point is that Liz, you, Carolyn, me — everyone should devote his or her time to doing what has meaning for them, or is enjoyable."

"You mean the minute something gets boring, we should drop it? If that's the case, I think I'll give up cooking," my mother said.

"Or I'd rather not go to school," Carolyn piped up.

"I agree with you there," I said.

"But that's not what I'm talking about. We all have responsibilities we have to live up to, but there are some things that we shouldn't impose on other people. For example, E.J., after one camping trip when we were first married, you said, 'never again.' Now, wouldn't it have been mean of me to insist?"

"Honey, you know how I am about outdoor plumbing." E.J. was smiling, and I was grateful to my father for changing her mood.

"And I don't like playing bridge, so you don't make me play it. Or is it because I'm such a bad player?"

"John, you just don't try. You'd be terrific if you'd concentrate."

"But I think it's a waste of time. I'd rather do a million other things that *you* might think are a waste of time."

"What are you getting at, Dad?" Carolyn said.

"I guess it's a roundabout way of saying that if Lizo wants to drop ballet and take up gymnastics, I think she should."

"You mean it?" I said, relieved that my father was on my side.

"Well, I'm not so sure," E.J. said. "I'm going to have to think it over. Why don't you take extra tennis lessons or something that will be important to you the rest of your life?"

I usually don't cry no matter how angry I get, but I had trouble keeping back the tears of frustration. My father spotted it immediately and tactfully said, "We don't have to decide this minute. Let's all sleep on it, and tomorrow we'll talk about it again."

"Good idea," E.J. agreed. "Now, who's ready for more?"

"Not me. I'm getting picked up in about twenty minutes and I've got to put on my face," Carolyn said.

"And leave me with the kitchen detail," I growled.

"Please," Carolyn pleaded. "I'll make it up to you."

"Go ahead," I sighed. "This just isn't my day. I might as well drown myself in dishwater."

"Thanks, Elizabeth, I won't forget."

"What are you going to do for me?"

"I'll get you a tumbling mat for Christmas."

As usual with Carolyn, I wasn't sure if she was being sarcastic, but I let it pass. At least if she was out, the phone would be free and I could call Tracy. *She* understands me.

# II _____

The next day we were going to the Nelsons' for Thanksgiving dinner. Amanda Nelson is one of E.J.'s best friends — they play bridge at least two afternoons a week. Amanda is one of these perfectly groomed women whose medium-length, light-brown hair always curves under the proper way, her fingernail polish is never chipped, and her skin is flawless. Amanda is really nice, although sometimes her gushiness is a little overdone.

Sam Nelson, her husband, is the robust, jolly salesman type. He's a space salesman for a radio station, and E.J. says he makes oodles of money. He's fun to visit but I wouldn't want to live with him. I mean he's *never* serious.

They have one daughter, Amanda the Second, who everyone calls Twosie. She's a real pain — the classic only child who's spoiled rotten. I suppose it's not her fault, because her parents keep telling her how great she is. She's in seventh grade, and maybe she'll improve with age. I have to admit she's pretty — a miniature version of Amanda — and I guess she's smart, because her parents never fail to mention that she's always getting A's.

We were expected at the Nelsons' at one o'clock. For the first time in ages, I put on my navy-blue pleated skirt and my embroidered Swiss blouse that I save for special occasions. I was just slipping into my dark-blue clogs when Carolyn wandered into my room, and headed for my bureau without even looking at me. "Can I borrow your white cardigan?" she asked.

"Sure," I told her, "if I can borrow your red one."

"It's a deal." She pulled my sweater out of the drawer, and then looked at me. "Hey, you look really good."

"Thanks," I said.

"You could stand a little eye shadow."

"You mean so I can turn on Sam?"

She laughed and strolled out of my room, saying, "You've got to start somewhere."

E.J. and Carolyn were still getting ready when I went downstairs. My father put down the magazine he was reading when I went into the den. It was the first time I'd been alone with him since last night's discussion.

He looked at me carefully, smiled, and said, "You look pretty."

"Thank you," I said, and sank into a corner of the couch. I didn't feel much like talking, which is kind of unusual around my father.

"What's wrong, Liz?" he asked.

"You know," I mumbled.

"You really want that gymnastics class, don't you?"

"Yep."

"Well, anything's possible."

"What does that mean?"

Before he had a chance to answer, E.J. stuck her head in the room and said, "We better get started." Then she backed out and called upstairs, "Hurry up, Carolyn, we're waiting for you."

My father walked over to where I was sitting, stuck his hand out to pull me up, and said in a low voice, "What I mean is, don't worry!"

"I'll try not to," I said.

We went into the kitchen where E.J. was wrapping a huge bottle of iced champagne in chef's foil. That was our Thanksgiving offering to the Nelsons. Every other year they brought us a bottle. I suggested that we skip the back and forth presentation, and that each family buy their own. E.J. said I missed the point. "Ritual is very important, and we couldn't walk in empty-handed. And everyone likes champagne."

"That's true," I said, thinking *she'd* missed the point of humor.

"Now, why don't you bring the car around, John, dear," E.J. instructed. "Carolyn and I will meet you out front."

"C'mon, Liz," my father said.

We went out the back door of the kitchen to the garage. On the way I said, "Do you think there's a chance that mother will change her mind?"

"There's always that chance. It's not as though you're asking to go in the astronaut program. And there's always the argument that the class is filled with young women, none of whom look like Arnold Schwarznegger, I'm sure."

"That's absolutely sure," I said, laughing. "In fact, the smaller the better, it seems to me, when it comes to gymnastics."

I was already feeling better as I climbed in the back seat of our Chevy. It's four years old and my father says it's time to turn it in, but I'm used to it and wouldn't feel comfortable in a brand-new car, especially because next year I'll be getting my learner's permit.

E.J. and Carolyn were waiting for us on the sidewalk in front of our house. My father pulled up to the curb and Carolyn piled in the back seat while Mother sat next to my father. As my father drove off, E.J. turned and looked at me. "You look sweet, honey," she said. "I just love seeing you in a skirt. You could wear a little makeup, though."

"How about me?" Carolyn teased.

"I told you before you looked lovely." She stared hard at Carolyn, and then frowned. "Did you add more mascara?"

"I think it's dramatic," Carolyn said haughtily.

"If you're going on the stage, it is. I think you've overdone it," E.J. said.

"Oh, Mother," Carolyn grumbled.

I was glad for a change that I wasn't getting picked on.

"Ask your father what he thinks," E.J. suggested.

"It's not worth arguing about," my father said.

"You're right, honey," E.J. agreed. "I just read an article about how children are individuals, and should be allowed to express themselves their own way, even if it's not exactly the way their parents would like them to behave."

"Right on, Mother!" Carolyn and I said in unison. Then we all burst out laughing.

I knew Carolyn was thinking she could use this argument to wear as much makeup as she pleased, or stay out as late as she wanted. I, of course, thought it justified my wanting to be a gymnast. But I didn't think this was an appropriate time to bring up the subject. After all, I didn't want to spoil Thanksgiving with a heavy discussion, and I sure didn't want to embroil the Nelsons in this.

## 12 _____

Amanda and Sam greeted us as though they'd just discovered an oil well in their backyard. No one would have believed that E.J. and Amanda had played bridge together two days ago.

The first thing Sam bellowed when we arrived was, "How's the second best-looking family in the country?" Then he laughed uproariously and gave my mother a bear hug first, and then me. When he came to Carolyn, he stood back and said, "Where did you get those eyes?" It was hard to tell if he was admiring them or making a crack about the mascara.

Before Carolyn could answer, he pounded my father on the shoulder with one hand and grabbed the bottle of champagne John was holding with the other. "We'll be needing this," he said.

Twosie managed to get in a few "hi's" and when she noticed my dark-blue clogs she pointed to them and shouted, "Mother, those are exactly the kind I want. I told you they came in blue."

"Yes, dear," Amanda said. "Maybe we'll get some on Saturday." I wondered then if anyone *ever* didn't give Twosie her own way.

Then we went into the living room where a large, friendly-looking woman, her graying hair pulled back in a bun, was standing. "This is Maggie, Sam's sister from Cincinnati," Amanda said. Then she introduced us, and Maggie shook hands with each one of us.

"She's great," Sam explained, still hanging on to the bottle of champagne. "Even though she's hooked on women's lib."

"Let's not get started," Amanda warned. "Why don't you just open the champagne."

"Good idea," Sam said, and started pulling out the cork.

"C'mon and help me get some champagne glasses, Twosie," Amanda said.

"Isn't that why Bella's here?" Twosie asked. Bella's the Nelson's housekeeper and I sometimes wonder why she stays with them. Probably Sam pays her extra or she wouldn't put up with Twosie.

Ordinarily I wouldn't want to act like a goody-goody but Amanda seemed embarrassed, so I walked over to her and said, "I'll help."

"You're a doll," Amanda said as I followed her into the hall, which leads to the dining room and then into the kitchen. Maybe I was imagining it, but I was sure I could hear Twosie say "Yech" as I walked past her sitting on the most comfortable chair next to the fireplace.

Bella is Viennese and every time she sees me she says the same thing. "How's my skinny Elizabeth?"

"Skinny as ever," I always say.

"Hope you eat something today," she scolded. "If you lived in this house you wouldn't get away with weighing ninety pounds."

"Ninety-five," I corrected.

Amanda handed me a tray of glasses and picked up a bowl of shrimp. "Bella," she said, "if we listened to you we'd never stop eating."

"You're safe," Bella snapped back, "because no one ever listens to me." Then she opened the oven, basted the turkey, and made it clear that the conversation was ended. It occurred to me then that Bella was very temperamental and a lot of people wouldn't put up with *her*. Maybe she was the perfect match for Twosie.

When we returned to the living room, E.J. was commenting on Amanda's plants. They were housed in a winterized porch off the living room, and Maggie said admiringly, "My sister-in-law has a green thumb. She really works magic with these plants." Then she turned to Amanda, who was putting the shrimp bowl on the coffee table. "Do you play Mozart or Bach for them, or just talk, Mandy?"

"Neither," Amanda insisted. "They just seem to grow."

"I don't believe it," Maggie protested. "I believe you have some special chemistry. I, on the other hand, seemed to have a brown thumb. I mean I sometimes think plants hate me."

"Well, you can't be good at everything," Sam said. "After all, you're one of your firm's top brokers — or is it brokeresses?"

Maggie shook her head and smiled. "Sam," she said, "I love you, but you're hopeless."

"Not hopeless, just old-fashioned. I believe . . ."

"Sam," Amanda interrupted, "can't we get
off the subject? That's all you can talk about
when Maggie visits us."

"You're right, Mandy, you're right. I'll drop
this heavy discussion and we'll concentrate on
the old bubbly."

Amanda handed each of us a glass and Sam
went around the room pouring. When everyone's
glass was filled, he turned to his sister. "Maggie,"
he said, "because you're our special guest, and
just to show there's no hard feeling, you propose
a toast."

"Why, thank you, Sam." She paused a few
seconds and then said, "First, I want to say how
happy I am to be sharing Thanksgiving with all
of you."

"And second?" Sam asked.

"And second, here's to the ERA!"

"You got me!" Sam said good-humoredly, and
then Sam went into the den off the living room,
and came back with his camera.

The first thing he did was show it to my father.
"Look at this baby, John. It's one of those new
special Nikons, with a built-in everything."

"It's a beauty," John said, genuinely impressed. Then the two men got into a serious
discussion about the merits of various cameras.

Amanda and E.J. were huddled in a corner
with Maggie, describing a bridge hand, while
Carolyn and I sat on the couch, digging into the
shrimp bowl. Twosie wandered over to where we

were sitting. She sank down next to Carolyn and stared at her eyes. "How do you get them like that?" she asked almost reverently. I realized then that Carolyn was the only person she seemed to treat with respect. Maybe she knew she couldn't push her around.

"It takes a lot of practice," Carolyn said in an offhand manner.

"They're terrific. My mother won't even let me wear eye shadow. Isn't that the pits?"

"Well, you are a little young," Carolyn said patronizingly.

"Oh, c'mon," Twosie groaned.

"I don't even wear lip gloss," I said.

Twosie looked at me and frowned. "That's your problem. You'll probably be like my Aunt Maggie. She wears hardly any makeup."

"I think she looks very good," I said, glancing at Maggie, who had strong classic features, and warm brown eyes.

"You would,'" Twosie said, not too pleasantly. I didn't bother to answer, and Carolyn gave me a knowing look. One thing Carolyn has taught me is that when someone tries to get a rise out of you by making a nasty remark, one of the best things to do is ignore it. That way it loses its significance. Sometimes it's hard to do, but it's almost always worth it.

"Smile," Sam said. He was on his knees in front of us, snapping away with the camera. "If I had to write a caption for this, I'd call it 'The Three Beauties.' "

"Oh, Daddy," Twosie groaned, "you think

everyone's beautiful." I think she figured that maybe she was the only one who deserved that adjective.

Then Bella appeared at the entrance to the living room, holding a fantastic-looking turkey on a silver tray decorated with love apples, parsley, and orange slices. "Here it is," she barked, but her eyes were smiling.

Everyone oohhed and aahhed and then Sam said, "Lemme immortalize that on film."

"Hurry up. My arms are breaking," Bella complained.

Sam quickly approached her and took a couple of pictures. Then my father offered to carry the tray, but Bella refused, and marched into the dining room.

"Another independent one," Sam muttered to my father as they followed her. "These women don't know what they're missing."

My father just chuckled. The rest of us trailed behind them and I thought Amanda was right. Sam was hooked on the subject. But everyone was feeling good now, and I figured there wouldn't be any serious debate at the dinner table.

# 13

Sam sharpened the carving knife with a flourish and then pointed it at the bird. *"En garde!"* he said, the knife poised in midair like a fencing sword. Everyone laughed except Amanda, who said, "Sam, stop horsing around. We're all starving."

"And everything else will get cold," Bella scolded as she served the steaming, homemade hot rolls.

"You're right, you're right," Sam said agreeably, and proceeded to carve the roast.

When everyone was served turkey and dressing, and the brussel sprouts, sweet potatoes, and cranberry mold was passed, Sam opened up another bottle of champagne. "Can't have too much of the good stuff," he explained as he offered some to everyone.

He went around the table. "I'll just wet the bottom of your glass," he explained. When he came to Twosie's, he poured out a thimbleful.

"That's not enough," Twosie whined.

"It's enough for a future ballerina. You have to keep in shape now with this new endeavor," Sam said, but I noticed he poured out a little more, probably to avoid a scene.

"Ballerina?" E.J. said.

"We've just decided it's time Twosie developed an outside interest, and I think ballet is so beautiful," Amanda told her.

"I agree," E.J. said promptly.

I could feel it coming. A floodgate had been opened, E.J. would have Amanda on her side, and my dreams about being a gymnast would be squashed.

"Annabella interviewed us last week and she said she could squeeze Twosie into the beginner's class in January. We're so pleased." Then Amanda turned to me. "You study with Annabella, don't you, Liz?"

"For the time being."

"What does that mean?"

"Well, I was thinking of switching."

"To what?" Twosie asked impatiently.

"Gymnastics," I answered, as evenly as possible.

"What on earth for?" Sam roared. "A delicate creature like you shouldn't get into that strenuous stuff."

"I'm not that delicate," I said, trying not to lose my cool, "and you can go at your own pace. If you don't overdo, it's not too strenuous."

"I happen to think it's a fascinating sport," Maggie said.

"For the fellows, maybe, but not for lovely

young ladies," Sam said. "Not if you want to be a perfect girl."

"Sam, you've got to be kidding," Maggie protested. "Gymnastics is one of the fastest growing sports for women. I love to watch it. If I had a daughter, I'd encourage her to take it."

"Another of your unisex ideas, Maggie."

"Not at all. You wouldn't think twice about Twosie taking tennis lessons, but I'm sure there was a time when that was considered strictly for men."

"I don't know about you, Maggie," Sam said, shaking his head.

"I happen to agree with Sam," E.J. remarked. "I can't imagine why anybody, man, woman, or child, would want to leap around like a bunch of wild chimpanzees."

"E.J.," my father said quietly, "that's hardly the case. Gymnastics is a very exacting sport. Sure it takes strength, but it also take a lot of grace."

"What do you think, Carolyn? You're a sensible young lady," Sam asked.

"That's a loaded question," Carolyn said, smiling. She's not afraid to speak her mind, I thought, and I was relieved when she said, "It's an okay sport. Not for me, though."

"And you, Mandy. What's your opinion?"

"Well, Sam, I hate to disagree with you, but I feel the same way Carolyn does — it's an okay sport. It wouldn't be for me, but maybe I'm old-fashioned. When I was in school all the girls took dance."

"That was certainly the way in the South," E.J. added.

"But then, E.J.," Amanda said smiling, "when we were young I'd never heard of gymnastics."

"You're right about that," E.J. admitted. "But somehow it turns me off."

"Have you ever *really* watched it?" my father asked.

"John, you always come up with the tough questions. You know I always switch to another channel or leave the room when there's a gymnastics exhibition."

"If you do watch it," Maggie intervened, "I can almost guarantee you'll change your mind. I'll never forget the first time I saw Olga Korbut. She was tiny, under five feet, wore her hair in pigtails — and was dynamite. You couldn't help but love her."

Maggie sounded so convincing that even E.J. had to bend a little. "I guess you're right. I haven't given it a fair chance."

For the first time, I thought maybe there was hope. I looked at my father, who was sitting across the table and he smiled and nodded his head slightly. Then I knew the first battle had been won.

I tried not to show how excited I was, but I sure didn't feel like eating. Bella cleared away the main course dishes and brought in two freshly baked pies, which she placed in front of Amanda.

"Pumpkin or mince?" Amanda asked, going around the table. I knew better than to refuse, but I couldn't wait till dinner was over. Then, as Sam was finishing off his second slice of pie, he announced that he was going to show slides of their trip to the Yucatán in Mexico last summer. He added, "Starring Twosie Nelson." I knew we were in for it! Seeing Twosie in person was tough enough, but to see her featured in a movie was unreal.

It took a while for Sam to set up the projector and screen in the living room, while we sat around the dining room table having coffee.

Finally he announced, "Okay, gang, show time!" and we straggled into the living room.

He'd pulled out some extra bridge chairs so we all had a place to sit, and proceeded to show slides, along with a running commentary. It was just as bad as I anticipated. The first shot showed Twosie climbing the steps of the plane. Then there were a zillion slides of Twosie and the ruins. I began to believe that if you've seen one ruin you've seen them all.

After the first five minutes, which seemed more like hours, I turned off my head. That's a trick I do when I'm really bored. Sometimes it gets me into trouble, like when our math teacher, Mrs. Tucker, who thinks and looks like a computer — she always wears a tailored gray suit with eight buttons — explains something for the tenth time and I turn off. If she switches to a new subject, I'm completely lost.

Now, since the room was dark, no one would notice if I closed my eyes and daydreamed. As Sam's voice droned on, I thought how lucky I was that Maggie's views on gymnastics were so persuasive; that Amanda and Carolyn were neutral; that my father was definitely on my side, and that E.J. was coming around. The only real opposing voice was Sam's, and I knew he didn't have that much influence with my mother. Things were definitely looking up!

Finally the lights came on, and after a lot of exclaiming about Sam's slides, everyone helped fold up the bridge chairs. There was some more chitchat and then E.J. said, "It's almost five o'clock. If we stay here much longer, we'll be here for the next show."

"And believe it or not, I have to go to work tomorrow. We're getting out a special report on nuclear waste and even though the office is officially closed, three of us are going in," my father said.

"You're obviously in the wrong business," Sam observed, and I thought he really does have a knack for saying the wrong thing.

We got up to say our good-byes. As Maggie extended her hand to me, she said how glad she was to meet me, and then added as she looked me straight in the eye. "Don't let anything stop you." Of course I knew what she was talking about.

*14*

On the way home E.J. grumbled about having had too much to eat, and Carolyn moaned that she was invited to a "turkey sandwich" party at Steve's, and I said I was going to a "leftover-sleepover" at Ellen's.

"It was a lovely Thanksgiving," E.J. said.

"I could have lived without those slides," Carolyn commented.

"Me, too," I agreed.

"Sam's a good guy, but not too sensitive sometimes," my father said. "And he certainly has strong opinions."

"So does his sister Maggie," E.J. observed.

"I think she makes a lot of sense," I said. "Especially about gymnastics."

"Elizabeth, honey, you are going to drive me crazy about this. I'd like to settle it once and for all. John, what do you really think? Should Elizabeth give up three years of ballet to begin something new that will lead nowhere?"

"E.J., if that's what she wants, why stop her?" my father answered.

"Oh, my sainted aunt," E.J. exclaimed. "I don't have a chance with you two. Why do I even try?"

"You mean I can switch?" I said breathlessly.

"Do I have a choice?" my mother said with a sigh.

"Oh, mother," I squealed, "thank you, thank you," and I leaned over to give her a peck on the cheek. At the same time I squeezed my father's shoulder. It was him I should be thanking, but some of my mother's Southern tact must have rubbed off on me, and I knew he'd understand if I didn't say anything.

I couldn't wait to tell Tracy and the first thing I did when we got home was make a beeline for the phone, and call her. She sounded genuinely enthusiastic and we spent a long time figuring out what strategy I should use in telling Annabella I was dropping out. Finally we figured the best thing was to be perfectly honest — that I'd learned a lot from ballet but felt it was time for me to try something new.

"Remember," Tracy reminded me, "Tomo said he'd fix it up with Annabella."

"That's right, but I'd be chicken if I didn't tell her myself. I know she has a class of younger kids on Monday. I think I'll go over there and tell her then. It's better than dropping a bombshell on Wednesday."

"Want me to go with you?"

"Thanks, Trace, I could use the moral support."

"What are friends for?"

"You're the best."

"And I'll be the only, if we don't get over to Ellen's soon."

"You're right. We just got home, but I can leave in two minutes."

"Me, too. And when we get there, I'll show you how to do a handstand pirouette."

"That'll be great. I know I have a lot of catching up to do."

"Don't worry. You'll do fine."

"I hope so."

When I hung up the phone in the kitchen I went into the den where my mother was working on a needlepoint pillow and my father was reading some scientific publications.

"Hi and good-bye," I said. "I'm off to Ellen's."

"Good-bye, honey, have a good time," E.J. told me.

My father looked up from what he was doing and said, "You look as though you're going to fly over to Ellen's house."

"I think I could," I answered, laughing.

"I'm happy you're so happy," my mother observed, "but I hope you're not going to take this new thing so seriously that you'll be disappointed."

"Don't worry," I said as I blew them a kiss and backed out of the room. Nothing could dampen my spirits, even my mother's warning.

I practically did fly to Ellen's, and as soon as she answered the door she looked at me and said, "You're in love."

"Not exactly," I told her. "It's just that I'm going to take gymnastics."

"You're what?"

"Taking gymnastics."

"And that's why you have that glow?"

"It's a long story, but the whole point is it's something I really want to do and I didn't think I'd be able to and now I can."

"Oh, that's perfectly clear. Come in and sit down because I think maybe you've flipped out. Everyone is in the family room."

The family room has everything — a standing bar at one end, a fireplace at the other, and a thick red shag rug on the floor. When I walked in, Jackie was sitting on a bar stool, applauding, and Tracy was walking on her hands.

"Hi, Liz," Jackie said.

"What's going on?" Ellen asked.

"Floor show," Jackie explained.

Tracy, still upside down, stretched her legs out in opposite directions parallel to the floor.

"This is a handstand with a perfect split," she announced.

"I'll never be able to do that," I said in awe.

She slowly lowered her legs and stood up. "Sure you will. It just takes practice."

"What is this new thing with you?" Jackie asked.

"It's hard to explain, but I didn't think E.J. would let me, and now she is, and I can't wait to get started."

"You're not making too much sense," Jackie said.

I noticed Ellen gave Jackie a raised eyebrow look and shrugged her shoulders.

"You don't understand," I said hopelessly.

"Guess not," Ellen said, somewhat bewildered. "Not to change the subject, but does anyone want something to eat?"

There was a collective groan, and then Ellen suggested we all look at TV. "We can see the highlights of the Macy's parade."

"Good idea," I said. Nobody else was ready to admit it, but that was something we still weren't too old to enjoy. Also, I thought maybe it would get me off thinking about gymnastics. I could see that no one except Tracy could understand my enthusiasm, and I could easily get to be a bore.

## *15*

The rest of the weekend dragged, mainly because I couldn't wait till after school Monday, when I'd go to the Y, find Annabella, and tell her my decision. Sometimes I think anticipating something you don't want to do is worse than actually doing it. I mean if you have to take a test or have a dentist's appointment, it's better to get it over with than think about it. I mentioned this to my father once and he said that's exactly what Shakespeare meant when he said, "A coward dies a thousand deaths, a brave man only once." Right now there was no question which category I was in!

As soon as the last bell rang, Tracy met me outside school and we hurried over to the Y. We arrived at the ballet room before any of the kids. Annabella was already there, one leg on the bench, studying her clipboard, which had a list of names she uses for attendance. She gave us the double take as we came in, and then said,

"Wrong day, Liz. Has the holiday upset your inner time clock?"

"Nope," I said, suddenly feeling tongue-tied.

"Do you want some extra practice today?"

"Nope."

"C'mon Liz, I haven't got all day. And who's your friend?"

"My name is Tracy. Liz is here to tell you her new plan."

Much to my relief, Annabella smiled. "Oh, yes," she said. "Does it have something to do with Tomo and gymnastics?"

"You guessed it," I shouted in astonishment.

"Not exactly, Liz. I happen to have seen Tomo in the cafeteria today and he mentioned to me that you spoke to him last week about switching to his class."

"It was his idea," I said defensively.

"He said you were a natural, and that your ballet training has been an excellent discipline."

I thought that Tomo was a good diplomat and had paved the way for me perfectly. "It's nothing personal," I said, not wanting to hurt her feelings.

"Don't worry, Liz. I'm not insulted. I'm always getting new students — some of them even recommended by Tomo."

"You mean you're not mad at me or anything "

"Of course not. Tomo says he's spotted you as having real potential. He says you could go all the way."

"Really?"

"Really. One thing, though, Liz. Don't forget me when you win your first competition."

"I'll never forget you," I said sincerely. I was about to say more, but half a dozen little kids had straggled into the room and Annabella changed into her super-strict manner, clapped her hands, and said, "All right, people. Take your positions at the barre."

As everyone scrambled into their places, I felt an unexpected pang of sadness, as though one phase of my life was over. I must have been transfixed, and then I heard Tracy say, "C'mon," and tugged at my elbow. Then she added in a whisper, "Mission accomplished."

"Coming," I said, and waved to Annabella who was so busy taking attendance that she didn't seem to see me.

"Good-bye, Annabella, and thanks," I said in a loud voice.

Then she looked up briefly from her clipboard and said, "Good luck, Liz."

I followed Tracy into the corridor. She stopped suddenly and looked at me. "Congrats," she said. "You've done it."

"Thanks, Trace. It was a lot easier than I thought it would be. Now, shall we tell Tomo?"

"Sure. He's probably in the gym."

We walked into the gym and looked around, but it was deserted. As we started to leave and headed for the front door, we spotted Tomo coming down the hall. "Hi," he said beaming. "What's the good word?"

"I can switch," I announced happily.

"Terrific," Tomo said. "This must be my good day."

"Why?" Tracy asked. "Just because you've captured Liz?"

"Well, that's one reason. But the other is because I just spoke to the director of the Y, and finally persuaded him that we must have gymnastics on a compulsory basis three times a week. It's going to be Monday, Wednesday, and Friday from four to five-thirty. As you know, Tracy, it was only compulsory once a week and only the more serious kids came extra days. Now the dilletantes can drop out. This is a serious business."

"You don't have to tell me," Tracy said. Then she turned to me. "You won't have a problem, will you, Liz?"

"I hope not."

"Who's stopping you?" Tomo asked.

"Nobody," I said determinedly. I'd gone this far, and nothing would stop me now.

"As long as you're here, why don't you put on your leotards, and Tracy will show you a few tricks."

"A private lesson?" Tracy said delightedly. "Come on, Liz. Let's change."

We raced down the steps to the locker room and hurriedly undressed. As I pulled up my bright red leotard, Tracy looked at me admiringly, and said, "That's a great color. You'll steal the show with that, even if you can't do anything. Next time, I'm getting a flashy leotard!"

"You look good in basic black," I observed. "It's very sophisticated."

"But not outstanding. Anyhow, let's get going. You don't know how lucky we are to get Tomo alone."

# 16

When we returned to the gym, Tomo was deeply involved in conversation with some guy from my school.

Tracy whispered to me, "Tomo's not exactly alone. But do you know who that is?" she asked excitedly.

"He looks familiar," I said.

"That's Roger Kimball. He's associate editor on the paper."

"Of course! That's why I know him!"

"Cute, huh?" Tracy asked.

"Not bad," I answered. "I wonder what he's doing here?" I said, thinking he really was cute. He was slim, had curly brown hair, brown eyes that had a perpetually amused look, and a spate of freckles on his nose.

"Let's find out," Tracy said and boldly walked over to where they were standing. I trailed behind her.

Tomo stopped short when he saw Tracy and said, "Hi. This is Roger Kimball."

Tracy asked, "Are you joining our gymnastics class?"

"I'd like to, if you two are part of the team," Roger said, smiling. I couldn't figure out why, but I could feel myself blushing and hoped it didn't show. To cover my embarrassment, I quickly said, "What are you doing here then?"

"I'm trying to line up some interviews with gymnasts."

"I've suggested he wait until it's closer to the time of the competition. Then he can talk to the final entries. They'd be the perfect ones to interview," Tomo told us.

"Good idea," Tracy said.

"Do you plan to enter the competition?" Roger asked her.

"Plan to," Tracy said, "but you never know."

"And you, Liz?" He seemed to be looking right through me.

"Don't know. This is my first day."

"Your first day? Well, you better get to work. I'll be back in a couple of weeks and see if you're still around."

"I hope I will be," I said, and could feel my cheeks starting to burn again.

"Thanks for seeing me, Tomo," Roger said. "I'll be back with a photographer in a couple of weeks."

"It'll be a sensational sports feature," Tomo said admiringly. "You obviously have excellent judgment."

"So do you," Roger said as he backed away, and I knew he was staring straight at me.

I didn't have time to think about that, though, because Tomo was saying, "I'll put on some music and you can do some warm-ups. No matter how great you feel, Liz, you always have to warm up." He walked toward the corner of the room where there was a record player.

"We warm up for at least fifteen minutes," Tracy explained, and stretched out on the floor.

"Okay, gang," Tomo instructed as he placed a record on the turntable. "We'll start with the *rock*."

"Tomo's got these cute names for everything," Tracy said, turning over on her stomach, "but the exes aren't always too cute."

I imitated her as well as I could — rolled over on my stomach, placed my palms on the floor next to my hips, and pushed my head and shoulders back until my arms were straight.

"Hold it," Tomo ordered. "Relax. Now five more times."

We did what he said, and then he told us to bend our legs up, catch our ankles, and rock back and forth.

"Lift your chest and thighs as high off the floor as possible. Now put your hands back on the floor in the original position, keep your legs bent, and try to touch the back of your head."

Next he had us doing sit-ups, backbends, bend-overs, and standing-up stretches. It all came easily, and I figured I was in good shape, thanks to Annabella.

"Can you do a handstand, Liz?" Tomo asked.

"I've been doing that since second grade," I bragged, and proceeded to show off.

I balanced myself on my hands, kicked my legs into the air, and then brought my legs together, convinced that I was doing it perfectly. Therefore, I was surprised to hear Tomo say critically, "No good. That might be okay in second grade, but not now. Your hands are too far apart from your shoulders, and your back is too arched."

He placed his hand on the small of my back and said, "Less bend here."

I did my best to straighten out and move my hands directly under my shoulders, but lost my balance in the process.

"Watch Tracy," Tomo instructed. And Tracy gracefully did a handstand.

"Looks perfect to me," I said.

"Almost a ten," Tomo estimated. "The index fingers should be pointing straight toward the front."

Tracy shifted the position of her hands slightly, and Tomo said, "Okay. That's good." Then he said to me, "The handstand is a basic stunt which should be perfected, because it's used as a part of a lot of gymnastic moves, and not just floor work. Also, it's a lot easier to learn technique correctly than unlearn a bad habit. Are you ready to try again?"

"Sure," I said enthusiastically.

"Remember, the space between your hands should be shoulder-width. Keep your head straight, so your ears are between your arms.

Tighten your hip muscles. Contract your upper body so that your ribs are pulled into your backbone."

I couldn't believe there were so many things to think about for what I considered a simple stunt. I tried again, trying to keep in mind all his pointers.

"Better," he said, "but still too much arch. Contract, contract, contract." He placed both his hands on my waist and I tried to pull in my ribs.

"Good," he complimented me, and moved away as I lowered my legs. "You can practice against the wall, and that will increase your endurance and technique. Also, you can practice at home."

"I will, I will," I promised. "That's the kind of homework I like."

"Now let's try some beam work," Tomo suggested. "One of the toughest things about the beam is getting on it properly. And nothing in a competition is more demoralizing than being penalized for a routine before you've even begun. You'll lose half a point."

I didn't have the foggiest idea about points, but I didn't want to appear stupid, so I thought I'd ask Tracy later.

"Tracy, show us the hitchkick mount."

"Sure," Tracy said, as we walked over to the beam.

I watched carefully as she swung onto the beam and held her balance. It didn't look that hard.

"Let me try," I said as Tracy jumped down. Then I tried to mount the beam the same way as Tracy and I flew right over to the other side. Tracy and Tomo both laughed, but I didn't think it was so funny.

"Not so fast," Tomo advised. "If you're not in complete control you'll never make it."

After three more tries, I managed to land dead center on the beam and keep from falling. Both Tomo and Tracy applauded. I spread my arms in order to keep my balance, and looked down. It seemed like an awfully long way to fall and I couldn't imagine doing any tricks from this height.

Tomo must have read my mind because he said, "That's enough on the high beam for your first time. I want you to come down now and later practice on the low beam — walking on your toes forward and backward, doing squat turns and pivot turns — until you feel at home on four inches."

"Okay," I said, and jumped down, hoping I didn't show how relieved I was.

"I've got time for one more trick. What'll it be, Tracy?"

"Let's vault," Tracy suggested.

"Okay. The first important thing here is how you approach the board. You run fast on the balls of your feet, and both feet should touch the board at the same time. That gives you the spring off the board and you squat and jump off. Demonstrate, Tracy."

Tracy ran easily, hit the board, and executed the move smoothly.

"Very good, Trace. Now you try, Liz."

I started my run but lost momentum and actually found myself stuck on the horse. Again, Tomo and Tracy burst out laughing, which I didn't appreciate.

"Try again," Tomo told me. "This is your first day, and you shouldn't be discouraged."

"Don't worry," I said, and went to the opposite end of the gym to begin my run.

This time I was going with enough force to squat on and jump off.

"That's good," Tomo said. "Now I think you've had enough for one day."

"I guess so," I said, reluctant to leave.

"I'll see you Wednesday, and don't forget to practice your handstand, Liz."

"Don't worry, Tomo. I'll rate a ten by Wednesday."

"I like your spirit," Tomo said.

"We'll see ya," Tracy said, and headed for the door.

"Bye, Tomo," I called as I hurried to catch up with Tracy. "Thanks for everything."

As we went downstairs to the locker room, I said to Tracy, "That was so much fun, even though it's not as easy as it looks."

"I knew you'd love it."

"And Tomo is the greatest."

"I told you."

"I can't wait till Wednesday."

"Hey, you're not going to get boring about this, are you?" I noticed a slight edge to Tracy's voice, and I thought maybe I was getting carried away.

"I hope not," I said. "Anyhow, I promise not to mention gymnastics once on the way home."

"Good," Tracy said lightly. Then I thought maybe I'd imagined her irritation, but to play it safe I decided to change the subject.

"How's your mother?" I asked, when we got to our lockers and began changing our clothes.

"Still going out with Dr. Friedman."

"Who's he?"

"A radiologist from the hospital. I've met him a couple of times and he seems nice. A little stuffy, but he tries hard."

"Aren't you glad she's going out?"

"Guess so. It's what I wanted."

"But?"

"But now I'm really alone a lot."

"You can always come over."

"Sure, Liz, but it's not the same."

"I know. Maybe, though, they'll get married and then you'll have a whole family."

"I'm already fifteen. It's too late for that."

"You've still got a few good years left," I said, trying to get her to laugh.

"I suppose," she said, almost smiling.

I looked at the clock on the wall and noticed it was after six. "Oh, oh," I squealed, "it's late and E.J. will kill me if I'm not home by six-thirty."

"You mean you didn't tell her you were coming to the Y to see about gymnastics?"

"Ssshhh," I warned, "don't use that word."

Then Tracy really did laugh and I felt for the time being, at least, things were back to normal.

# 17————

When I arrived home, I was surprised to see Carolyn alone in the kitchen. She was boiling water in a large kettle that we use for spaghetti and sautéing some meatballs in a frying pan.

"Whew," I gasped. "I raced home because I didn't want to get in trouble and nobody's here. Thank goodness!"

"I'm here, Elizabeth, and you're supposed to be helping me."

"Where are they?"

"Mother finally convinced Daddy that he needed a new coat, and since the stores are open late tonight they went shopping. E.J. called about an hour ago and said we should start making dinner and they'd be home at seven at the latest."

"What can I do?"

"Make the salad."

"Sure," I said, and got all the ingredients out of the fridge. I sliced the tomatoes and was chopping the lettuce when I heard the car pull into the driveway. Then E.J. and John came in the back door.

"You girls are dreamy," E.J. exclaimed. "What would I do without you?"

"They obviously take after their mother," John remarked.

They were both in a really good mood, and I was wondering why. Usually shopping makes my father grumpy.

"Was your shopping successful?" Carolyn asked.

"Very," E.J. answered. "Your father got a beautiful, lined raincoat. Even he admits he likes it."

"It must really be beautiful. I've never seen you happy buying clothes," I said.

"That's not the real reason he's so happy," E.J. said as she followed my father into the hall, where they took off their coats and hung them in the closet.

When they came back to the kitchen she took a bottle of red wine out of the cupboard and said, "Here, John. We'll have a really good French wine."

"To celebrate buying a coat?" Carolyn asked in amazement.

"Not exactly," E.J. said. "Your father has been asked to do a series of articles on nuclear plants for a scientific journal."

"That's wonderful!" I shouted.

"Congratulations!" said Carolyn. "Does that mean you'll be rich and famous?"

"Neither. It's just means that all these reports

I've been doing on the dangers of nuclear waste will get a lot more exposure."

"Don't be modest, John. You were also told that one of the more popular family magazines might pick up your articles."

"And they pay more, right?" Carolyn asked.

My father chuckled and said, "You've got a one-track mind, Carola. But then, that's not always such a bad way to be."

All the time we were getting things ready, I was trying to figure out how to get in the fact that I would be taking gymnastics three times a week. I didn't want to make it sound like a big deal.

When we were finally all seated in the dining room, E.J. said, "How was school today?"

"I got a B on my French exam, much to my surprise," Carolyn said. "I was really worried about that."

"Wonderful," my father said.

"Good things are happening to everyone today," E.J. remarked.

"What's new with you, Liz?" my father asked.

I took a deep breath and said, "I had my first gymnastic class. Actually, it was just me and Tracy. Tomo showed us a few moves."

"And you're still in one piece," my father observed.

"Today's Monday. I thought it met every Wednesday, like ballet." E.J. sounded surprised.

"As a matter of fact," I said as casually as possible, "it's going to meet three times a week."

"Three times . . ." E.J. started to say, but

before she could even finish her sentence my father interrupted.

"That's probably a good idea. There's no way you can excel at a sport if you only work out once a week. I think three times is the minimum."

E.J. shrugged her shoulders. "If you say so," she sighed, "far be it from me . . ." and her voice trailed off.

"Let's have some more wine," my father suggested.

"Good idea," E.J. said, and passed her glass to be filled.

When supper was over Carolyn and I started clearing the dishes while my father and mother went into the den. I was in a semi-daze, thinking about how lucky I was that I didn't get in a hassle with E.J. The phone rang, and Carolyn grabbed the receiver. "This is an important call," she whispered to me, her hand over the mouthpiece. "I'll take it upstairs. Hang up for me, will you?"

"Okay."

"And I'll do the pots. Save them for me."

"Don't worry," I said as she skipped out. I was feeling so good about life that I would have scrubbed the walls without protesting.

I hardly had time to rinse off the dishes before putting them in the dishwasher when Carolyn shuffled into the kitchen. Her face looked blotchy, the way it gets when she's really upset. She's like me, though, and never wants anyone to see her cry.

"What's wrong?" I asked.

"You wouldn't understand," she growled.

I hate that kind of answer, but I could afford to be generous, so all I said was, "I saved the pots for you."

"Thanks a heap," she said sulkily.

"Listen, I'll help if you want, but then I have to practice my handstands."

"Your what?"

"My handstands. I've been doing them wrong all these years."

"Oh, Elizabeth, you're so lucky. Your needs are so simple."

"Are you kidding? Just because I don't have love problems . . . You must have had a fight with Steve." I've noticed that if I don't ask Carolyn direct questions, she tells me things. It worked this time too.

"Not exactly a fight," she admitted, "but I hinted strongly about going to the Christmas play, which is only three weeks off, and he didn't even ask me."

"Maybe you were too subtle."

" 'Fraid not. Also, we always plan to go out on Saturday night, and now he tells me he can't." Carolyn was attacking a pot furiously, and I thought the best way to get things clean is when you're mad.

I didn't think this was the appropriate time to point that out. Instead I said, "You can always go with someone else."

"Sure. So can he."

"Is that what's bothering you?" I asked, forgetting my indirect approach.

"Go stand on your head," Carolyn growled.

"My hands, my hands," I said, shaking them in the air.

"Same thing." Then she seemed to soften a little. "Look, I know you mean well, but I don't want to talk about it now. You'll find out if you ever fall in love."

"That'll be the day!" I said, and turned to leave.

"It'll happen," she assured me. "And you'll have *me* to talk to."

"I'll count on it, but right now I have to worry about getting the arch out of my back."

"Huh?"

"You wouldn't understand," I said, and hurried out of the kitchen.

I was halfway up the stairs when Carolyn called after me, "That's what I call getting even!"

# *18*

On Wednesday Tracy and I had arranged to meet outside school so we could go to the Y together. She was about ten minutes late, and I was getting more and more impatient.

"It's about time," I grumbled when she appeared.

"Sorry," she said abruptly. "I had to get *Lord of the Flies* out of the library for English. It's on the reserved list, and if I didn't get it today, I might never."

"I forgot about that," I said. "Will you let me have it when you're finished?"

"I'll bring it to you, but you'll have to sign for it."

"Okay, but let's hurry now. I don't want to be late my first day." I started to walk swiftly.

"Take it easy, Liz. We'll get there soon enough."

"I thought you were as enthusiastic as I am about gymnastics."

"Enthusiastic, yes, but not so compulsive."

"It's just that it's all so new to me."

"If you're that anxious, we'll jog over," she said amiably.

"Thanks," I said grinning, and set the pace.

When we got to the Y, we hurriedly changed and raced upstairs to the gym. All the kids were there bunched around Tomo, who was explaining the new schedule. I was relieved to see that the action hadn't begun. When he finished telling about the necessity of serious gymnasts working out three times a week, he gestured toward me and said, "This is our most recent acquisition, Liz Nelson."

Everyone turned to stare at me and there were a lot of hi's, and I was beginning to feel really self-conscious, but that didn't last long because Tomo said, "Let's get started."

We all spread out, Tomo put on a popular record, and then led us in a series of arm swings, stretches, curl ups, splits, and bridges. Next Tomo divided us into groups. He pointed to me, Tracy, and a girl named Jeanne Amster. She was a small, trim blonde who wore her hair in two pony tails, which made her look a couple of years younger than she was. The minute she discovered we were practicing together she introduced herself and said her birthday was next month, she would be fifteen, and that meant she would be entering the state competition in the fifteen-and-up group. "If I ever get that far," she added.

"I don't know anything about competitions," I confessed.

"I'll explain it all. First there's the local . . ."

Before she could continue, Tomo looked toward us and said, "You work on the low beam. Practice your pivots, forward and backward rolls, your squat turns. Liz, you must get comfortable working on a four-inch surface. Stand, turn, walk, sit on it."

"I understand," I said, nodding.

"Can I try my handstand on the low? I think I'm ready," Jeanne inquired.

"Go ahead," Tomo said encouragingly. "I think you're ready, too. If you feel good about it, you can try it on the high beam later. But wait for me, then, to spot you."

"Don't worry, Tomo," Jeanne promised. "I'm not crazy."

"Let's go," Tracy urged, putting her hand on my shoulder, and we walked over to the low beam.

"It's a cinch when the beam's on the floor," Jeanne explained as she showed me the way to do a squat, her arms forming a crown position over her head. Then she did a squat turn. "Get on," she said, "and follow my moves. Tracy will tell you what's wrong."

I got on the low beam and did exactly what she did.

"That's amazingly good," Tracy complimented me.

"It's like my *pliés* in ballet, so it's easy. I don't know if I can manage on the high beam."

"Don't worry about it," Jeanne said comfortingly. "We always have extra mats on the floor to cushion our falls in the beginning. And then you really get used to it."

Tracy stepped up on the beam and said, "This is how to do a turn." She shifted her body smoothly and it looked simple. But when I tried it, I lost my footing and was grateful the beam was on the floor.

"Try again," Tracy advised. "The trick is to grab the beam with your toes to steady yourself, and turn everything at once so you're properly centered."

I tried again, and this time was successful. "That's really good," Jeanne said. "You learn fast."

My confidence was increasing and along with Tracy and Jeanne I practiced doing splits and even some rolls. I had just come out of a backward roll when I saw Tomo approaching us. "How's she doing?" he asked.

"Terrific," Jeanne volunteered.

"Not bad for a beginner," Tracy added.

"Let's go over to the high beam now," Tomo said. "The mats are stacked up on each side so you can't hurt yourself."

"Great!" I said, thrilled with all the encouragement.

"First let me show you my handstand," Jeanne said to Tomo.

"Go ahead."

Jeanne then balanced herself on her hands and Tomo praised her. "You're ready for the high."

"Can I try it here?" I asked.

"Of course," Tomo said.

I did a handstand, stretching my body as much as possible, and being aware of keeping the arch out of my back.

"You've been practicing," Tomo commented. "I think you're ready to try the high, too."

"You mean it?" I yelped, and followed them to the high beam.

Jeanne and Tracy went first and then it was my turn. Since the mats were stacked halfway up the height of the beam, it wasn't too scary and I concentrated on my form. "That's fine," Tomo observed. "Next time, we'll reduce the number of mats even more, and before you know it you'll feel secure with just the floor beneath you. Take a five-minute break now and then come over to the bars."

The three of us wandered to the bars, while Tomo went around to the other groups, telling them what to do next.

"Do you want to enter any competitions?" Jeanne asked me.

"I haven't even thought about it," I replied.

"You can, especially if Tomo thinks it's a good idea," Tracy interjected. "He's already suggested that Jeanne and I enter the local meet in January."

"I'll never be ready for that," I whined.

"You never know," Jeanne said brightly. "Tomo says it's good to set goals for yourself. We'd be competing in the Class Three compulsory. That's the least advanced class."

"In the local meet you must get a score of twenty-eight to qualify for the sectional," Tracy said. "And in the sectional you must score a thirty to get into the state."

"I don't even know about scoring," I admitted.

"That's not hard. A score of ten is perfect. Tomo has a list of how everything is valued. The judges take off points if your underwear is showing," Jeanne said, and we all giggled.

"The bars are free now. Let's get going," Tracy urged.

We took turns doing a cast, a pullover, and a back hip circle. The last was the most fun, and I couldn't believe I could circle backward around the bar. I didn't want to stop, but Tomo announced it was time to go and that we should take hot showers when we got home to avoid muscle cramps.

The session ended at five-thirty. It was the fastest ninety minutes I'd ever experienced. I would have liked to go on but when I got downstairs and changed my clothes, my body did feel tired.

In the locker room some of the girls went out of their way to tell me how good I was, considering it was my first day. Ginger, who was slightly overweight and wore glasses, but was especially friendly, told me she'd taken gymnastics for a year and still couldn't do a decent back hip circle. "I still love it," she added, "and my mother thinks it will improve my figure."

I didn't know how to respond to that, so all

I said was, "The good thing about gymnastics is you can always improve your own technique and your own score. It's not like beating someone in tennis."

"I guess you're right," she said. "If I can manage a handstand by Christmas, I'll be satisfied."

Everyone around us laughed, and I could tell immediately that Ginger was one of the most popular girls. She was able to laugh at herself, and that made her totally likable.

On the way home, my head was buzzing with excitement. I didn't want to keep talking about it to Tracy, but she could tell I was preoccupied. "What are you thinking?" she finally asked after we'd been walking for about five minutes in silence.

"Don't kill me if I tell you, but I was thinking about what I could practice at home. I think maybe I'll get my father to make a beam I could use on the floor."

"You really are hooked," Tracy observed. "I think maybe I've created a monster."

"You can use it, too," I offered.

"No thanks," she said. "Enough's enough."

Then we said good-bye to each other and I walked the rest of the way home, wondering if I could possibly be ready to enter the competition in January.

When I got home, my father was alone in the kitchen, preparing his specialty, chicken cacciatore. He loves to cook, especially when he has a lot on his mind. He says it's a form of therapy.

And my mother claims we can't accuse her of being completely old-fashioned because there's nothing she likes better than having a home-cooked meal à la John — something unheard of when she was growing up in Atlanta.

I kissed my father on the cheek while he was browning some mushrooms. He glanced at me briefly and said, "What's happened? You look like a lit-up Christmas tree."

I never can hide my feelings — good or bad — but I never have trouble talking about the good ones.

"I've just had gymnastics, and it went so well. Even some of the other kids told me how good I was for a beginner."

"That's wonderful, Liz. But remember, sometimes you reach one plateau very early, and then it's really tough work to break through to another."

"I know. That's why I want to be able to practice at home, and that's why I thought maybe you could make a beam that I could use on the floor."

"That's very possible," he agreed, dumping the mushrooms over the chicken. "You give me the exact dimensions and I'll see what I can do."

"Terrific!"

"Now you should get ready for this elegant repast. Countdown is in exactly thirty minutes, and if you're smart, you'll take a hot shower after all that exercise. It will keep you from having sore muscles."

"That's exactly what Tomo told us. How do you know so much about 'reaching plateaus' and 'hot showers'?"

My father chuckled. "Why do kids think their parents have so much to learn all the time?"

# 19————

The next few weeks I was still in a state of euphoria about gymnastics. My father was right, though. I reached a plateau very early, and mastered the Class Three compulsory routine well enough so that Tomo suggested I definitely enter the local competition. The day he told me, Jeanne and I were practicing our floor routine, and I whispered to her the good news. She let out a yelp, slapped me on the back, and said, "That's wonderful!"

"Sshh," I cautioned. "I don't want to make a scene."

"I know what you mean," she said softly. "There are too many kids who have been working hard who aren't ready yet to enter a competition."

"That's exactly what I was thinking," I said.

I showed marvelous restraint, I thought, because I didn't tell Tracy until we were walking home together. "Tomo says I should enter the competition in January," I blurted out, as soon as Tracy and I were alone.

"I'm not surprised," she said coolly. "He's been spending enough time on you." I hadn't realized it until she said so, but Tomo actually had been devoting more time to me than to any of the others.

Still, her remark bothered me, but I brushed it off, saying, "That's because I had a lot of catching up to do."

"Well, I don't really think it's fair. We're all anxious to improve, and he should divide his time equally."

"Now that I'm almost caught up, he probably will." I was hurt that Tracy didn't seem at all glad that I would be entering the local, but I didn't say so.

"You've more than caught up," she said sarcastically.

"I'm having plenty of problems with the bars."

"I'm sure Tomo will help you get over them."

"The bars or the problems?" I asked lightly, hoping she'd get out of her bad mood.

"Really, Liz, the subject is beginning to wear thin."

"Sorry," I said. "We'll declare a moratorium. I promise to lay off talking about it, but it doesn't mean I won't practice." I was hoping she'd realize I was trying to be funny, but that backfired, too.

"You can practice all you want. Just don't tell me about it."

"Okay," I said. "I guess if my best friend tells me to cool it about something, I'd better listen. Right?"

"Right."

"You are my best friend, you know," I said, suddenly feeling very insecure. We had come to the intersection where we went in opposite directions, and I felt I had to say something that would reassure me about our relationship.

"Sure," Tracy said, evenly, and turned to go home. "See ya," she added, without looking back.

"So long," I said, no longer high from the good news. The rest of the way home I kept going over our conversation. *I guess if my best friend tells me to cool it about something, I'd better listen. Right? You are my best friend, you know. / Sure. See ya.*

When I got home, everyone was in the kitchen. I waved hello and then bolted upstairs to take a shower. I had so many mixed feelings that I couldn't talk about. I just wanted to be alone.

I threw off my clothes in the bathroom and turned the shower on full blast. I guess I was under a lot of tension, because unexpectedly the tears poured down my face along with the spray from the shower. I shampooed my hair, rinsed in cold water, and when I dried off, and put on clean jeans and a fresh shirt, I felt a lot better.

I was still nagged by Tracy's attitude, but I figured maybe she had the blahs. After all, she was the one who encouraged me in the first place. I was going to act as though everything was the same between us. It wasn't anything I wanted to talk about.

At dinner, I mentioned that I was planning to enter the local competition. I tried to make the announcement as low-key as possible because I didn't want to upset E.J., but even as I said it I could feel butterflies in my stomach. Fortunately no one asked too many questions, and most of the conversation revolved around Carolyn, who had been elected to do the decorations for the Christmas dance. That gave us an opportunity to make a lot of suggestions and I volunteered to help make popcorn balls.

After dinner Jeanne Amster called me. She enthused again about my entering the local and asked if she could come over and practice on the beam I told her my father had made for me.

"Any time," I said.

"Is Saturday okay?"

"It's fine. Come in the morning and stay for lunch."

"Wonderful! I'd much rather practice with someone than alone."

"Me, too."

When I hung up, it flashed through my head that I wished Tracy would come, too, but I knew she frowned on what she called my "eager beaver" attitude and I wanted to keep as laid back as possible.

I certainly wasn't trying to hide anything, but I thought it would be wise not to mention to Tracy that Jeanne was coming over. I guess I was afraid she'd make some snide remark and I didn't want another scene.

It was strange, I thought. Up to now it was E.J.'s attitude I'd been concerned about. I never thought I'd have to worry about Tracy's. I'd always confided in Tracy, but now I wasn't even allowed to talk about the most important thing in my life. Was this another example of a changing relationship that we discussed in our Human Relations class? I couldn't believe it could happen to Tracy and me, and I was determined to not let it happen.

# 20⎯⎯⎯⎯⎯⎯

On Saturday Jeanne appeared at our house about ten o'clock, and we immediately went into the cellar where we keep the washing machine and drier. The cellar is completely unfinished, but it's warm and it has plenty of floor space. My father had put the finished beam down there and told me that now he was inspired to fix up the room. Before Jeanne arrived I helped him unroll an old nine-by-twelve rug that we never used, and lay it on the floor.

"Not exactly beautiful, but it's better than working out on cement," I told Jeanne as she glanced around the cellar.

"It's perfect," she said, "and there's so much space!"

Jeanne had worn a leotard under her clothes, and I was already in mine, so we went right to work. Work isn't the right word because we horsed around a lot. It was so much fun that we lost track of time.

We were facing each other, doing splits on the beam and giggling because our toes would touch and Jeanne was so ticklish she had trouble keeping her balance. Then once, when she wasn't ready for it, I wiggled my toes against her foot and she laughed so hard that she actually did fall off. We both cracked up and then we heard footsteps coming down the stairs.

To my amazement, it was Tracy. I was shocked to see her, and I guess my jaw dropped and I didn't know what to say.

Jeanne, at least, had the presence of mind to say, "Hello, Tracy. You're just in time. We've warmed up the beam for you."

"I didn't know *you* were here," Tracy said in a steely voice.

"Why's that so surprising?" Jeanne snapped.

I was really embarrassed, but recovered enough to say, "Hey, why don't you stay for lunch?"

"No, thanks," Tracy refused. "I've got some things to do. The only reason I'm here is to drop off *Lord of the Flies*. Remember, Liz, you did ask me to."

"Oh, thanks," I said. "I know we have to do a paper on it before Christmas vacation."

"Do you think you'll ever find time?" she asked sarcastically.

"You know I always wait till the last minute on these things."

"That's your style, I guess. It's not mine." She started to go up the stairs.

"Hey, wait up," I shouted. "We're just going

to have cold cuts and stuff. There's some bologna — your favorite."

"I can't," she insisted. "I've got to find a birthday present for my mother. Her birthday's on Monday, and this is my last chance."

"Buy it after lunch. There'll still be plenty of time."

"Unlike you, I don't like waiting till the last minute," she shot back, and disappeared up the stairs.

Jeanne looked at me, raised her eyebrows, and shrugged her shoulders. "What's bugging her?" she asked.

"I'm not sure," I answered. "I like to think it's nothing I've done, but it's hard to tell. She won't come out and say it."

"If you ask me, she's jealous," Jeanne said, slipping into her jeans.

"Of what?"

"Of me being here, for starters. She wonders why you didn't invite her, too."

"I would have, but she's not nearly as interested as we are in gymnastics. In fact, she's made it clear that I should stop talking about it."

"Did it ever occur to you that you're better than she is at it, and now she's sorry she ever asked you to join Tomo's class?"

"That's dumb. I'm not better."

"Think about it a minute. You can already do a perfect squat vault on the horse, and your beam routine is probably better than hers."

"But I'm still scared to do much on the uneven bars. I think Tracy's a whiz on them."

"Right. But the way you're going, you'll catch up, and probably pass her."

"I didn't think of gymnastics as a sport where you had to beat someone."

"Not exactly. But you know there's a difference in ability. Otherwise, the whole class would be entering the local, not just you, me, and Tracy."

"You're right about that, I guess. I just wish you were wrong about Tracy."

"One other thing. Tracy was definitely Tomo's pet before you came along. He can't seem to help showing favoritism, although he's really nice to everyone. I think it has something to do with wanting to coach someone he believes can make it to the top. Before you, it was Tracy."

"What about you?"

"I just don't have it. My talk about entering the state competition is pure fantasy. But I love it so much that it doesn't matter."

"And you were never jealous of Tracy?"

"Why should I be? Besides, she's not my best friend."

Jeanne had finished dressing and followed me upstairs to the kitchen. I started pulling cold cuts out of the fridge, thinking hard about what she had said.

"I hope I didn't say something I shouldn't," Jeanne said apologetically after a heavy silence. "Sometimes I talk too much."

"No," I said slowly. "It made me see things a new way, that's all. And it's sort of a shock."

"I have a way of doing that," Jeanne beamed. "I'm constantly analyzing my brother's love life.

He's a freshman in college, and he comes to me for advice — or at least he pretends to."

"That's terrific."

"He says I should be a psychologist."

"Maybe you should. You've certainly opened my eyes."

"And I think all I've done is state the obvious."

"Meaning?"

"Meaning Tracy's your best friend. She's asked you to join something where she's been a star, and now you're outshining her."

"And she's angry."

"Exactly."

"What do I do now?"

"Well, you certainly shouldn't feel guilty. You should do your own thing."

"That's exactly what my father would say."

"He must be very intelligent," Jeanne said, laughing. "But enough of this. The session is over, and for all this advice, do you think you might be able to scrounge up some mustard?"

"It's a possibility," I said.

"And relish, maybe?"

"Why not," I said, pulling a crock of mustard and a jar of relish out of the fridge.

"See," Jeanne said as she piled a mixture of cold cuts on some rye bread and proceeded to spread mustard and relish on top, "anything's possible."

"You're right," I agreed. And although I still felt funny about Tracy, I knew once and for all I would have to do my own thing.

# 21 _____

There were six weeks left until the January competition, and on Friday Tomo pulled me aside and said, "Liz, I've been watching you these past weeks. You've got the strength and suppleness to be first rate — even Olympic material."

I could feel my face flush with excitement. "You mean it?" was all I could say.

"I've never said this to any of my other students."

"What do I have to do?" I asked idiotically.

"Work, work, work. Three times a week isn't enough. You'll have to come every day."

"Weekends, too?"

"If you want to go all the way. But I want you to think about it. I know you've got the potential, but it will take enormous drive and dedication to realize it."

I felt heady with everything Tomo was saying, and instinctively responded, "I want to, honestly."

"Don't give me a fast answer. You must think about it carefully. You'll have to make sacrifices along the way — some that you can't even anticipate."

"I'll think about it," I promised.

"Good. Now I've got to get back to the others."

"And I've got to work on the uneven bars. The Mill Circle Catch is still giving me a problem."

"Go to it," Tomo said. "And on Monday you can tell me your decision."

"Okay," I said, but I was already sure what my answer would be. I knew I'd have to make sacrifices, but I didn't know they would start that very same day!

I went over to the bars where Tracy had been working out. She was waiting her turn, and I stood next to her.

"Hi," I said casually.

"What was that all about? You and Tomo looked very serious."

I didn't want to lie, but I figured I could hedge a little. "Tomo says I should spend more time working out if I really want to improve."

"You mean he's going to give you private lessons."

"Not exactly. He just wants me to practice more."

"Are you planning to enter the Olympics?" she asked.

I wasn't sure if she was serious, so I answered, smiling, "Why not?"

Then it was her turn on the bars, and we stopped talking. After she completed her routine, she said she was going over to practice on the horse.

I was alone at the bars, and grateful for the opportunity to take my time, since no one was waiting for me to finish. I chalked up my hands and did a number of swinging movements, concentrating on releasing the low bar and catching the high bar for a Mill Circle Catch. I was so determined to get it right that I must have tried too many times because my palms started to bleed. I tried to ignore them but my hands stung so much I had to stop. Then Tomo blew his whistle, and announced that it was five-thirty.

"Have a good weekend," he said, as the class wandered toward the door. On my way out he stopped me and said, "Think it over carefully, and make sure you do what *you* want. Whatever you decide, remember it's for yourself, not anyone else."

"I will," I promised.

When I got downstairs, Tracy was already half dressed.

"I've got to wash my hands off," I told her. "They're actually bleeding."

"Yech," she said, as I disappeared into the girl's washroom. I ran cool water over my hands and blotted them dry with a paper towel. It only took me a few minutes, but when I went back to my locker, Tracy was no longer there, and her locker was closed. I was stunned, because we always waited for each other.

"What happened to Tracy?" I asked Ginger, trying not to show how upset I was.

"She said to tell you she couldn't wait because her mother expected her to meet her at the hospital and she had to rush home and change her clothes first."

"Oh," I said, noncommittally, thinking she could have told me herself, and that I would have hurried if she had asked me to. My feelings were really hurt.

I finished dressing in a daze, and then walked home alone. It was that time of year when it gets dark early, and there was the first chill of winter in the air. My mood blended perfectly with the bleak atmosphere.

I wanted to make sure my mother didn't see my hands, but the fates were really against me that day! When I let myself in the back door, my mother was struggling with a package she was wrapping.

"Elizabeth, honey, you're just in time. I'm trying to wrap these homemade jellies to send to Granny. I should have done it long ago if they are going to reach her for sure by Christmas. Take off your coat and let me borrow a finger. And incidentally," she added smiling, "hello."

"Hi," I said, dumping my coat on the kitchen chair. Then I gritted my teeth and gingerly removed my gloves, hoping E.J. wouldn't notice my sore hands. But I should have known better, because as soon as I tried to open my hand, I couldn't help saying "ouch." E.J. stared at me, glanced at my hands, which she grasped with her own, and turned them over so she could see my palms. "Heaven help us!" she shrieked. "What have you done to yourself?"

"It's not serious," I groaned. "It's from working on the bars."

"Your hands look like they've been through a meat grinder."

"They just have to get callused. It'll take a few days."

"And in the meantime, you probably can't hold a fork or a pencil."

"C'mon, mother, it's not so awful. Every ballet dancer's toes bleed."

"Elizabeth, I don't know about you," she said, shaking her head. Then she went to the cupboard and got out a box of boric acid and poured some into a bowl of warm water. "Sit down and soak," she ordered. "I'll hang up your coat."

Just as she went into the hall, my father came in the back door. "What's going on?" he asked, looking at me soaking my hands.

"Elizabeth's ripped her hands apart doing that crazy gymnastics," E.J. shrieked as she ran back into the kitchen. "Show your father."

I held up my hands like a sick puppy trying to beg, and that's exactly how I felt. Between my stinging palms and E.J.'s hysteria it was all I could do from bursting into tears.

"I think you'll live," my father said, smiling. "Now, can anyone say 'hello' at least."

"Hello, dear," E.J. said abruptly, and my father kissed her on the cheek.

"Hello, Daddy," I sighed.

"Back to your poultice," he ordered, and gave me a peck on the forehead.

My mother followed him into the hall, and I could hear her muttering. I knew she was talking about me and I just hoped my father would do a good job of defending me.

I was brooding about what a bummer life can be when Carolyn appeared.

"What are you doing?" she asked.

I held up my hands so she could see the damage. They were no longer bleeding, but looked red and swollen.

"Disgusting!" she said unsympathetically.

That did it! I leapt up from the kitchen chair and bolted upstairs, the tears flooding my face. I slammed the door to my room, threw myself on the bed, and wept.

A short time later there was a knock on the door and before I could muster enough energy to say, "Stay out," Carolyn walked in.

"Hey," she said gently, "I'm really sorry. I didn't know you were so sensitive about your hands. They'll get better."

"It's not my hands. It's everything."

"We all have days like that. Like everything bad happens at once."

"Not to you."

"That's what you think. Anyhow, Mother and Daddy say you should come down and have some dinner."

"I couldn't possibly. I'd throw up."

"In that case you better not. I'll relay the message. I just hope they don't kill *me*, which I learned today is what the Greeks did when a messenger delivered bad news to the rulers."

I knew she was trying to cheer me up, but the way I was feeling nothing would have worked.

At least I didn't have to face dinner. I dragged myself off the bed and took a hot bath. As I soaked in the tub and stared at my hands, I thought about the "sacrifices" Tomo talked about. Already gymnastics had caused my best friend to reject me, my mother to be angry, and Carolyn to tease me. And this was only the beginning.

After my bath I collapsed into bed and fell asleep almost immediately. I guess I was emotionally exhausted, and when I woke up the next morning, after sleeping around the clock, I still felt glum.

I wasn't in the mood to talk to anyone and I was glad that when I went into the kitchen to pour some cereal and milk into a bowl, no one was around.

I was still sitting at the kitchen table when E.J. came in and said, "Good morning, Elizabeth. Carolyn and I are going to do some Christmas shopping. Do you want to come along?"

"No, thanks," I told her.

Then Carolyn stuck her head in. "You know Elizabeth likes to wait till the last minute."

"That's right," I answered, concentrating on my cereal. I knew they were both trying to act as though nothing unusual had happened the night before, but I couldn't seem to snap out of my bad mood.

"We'll see you later, then," E.J. said.

I nodded.

After they left I cleaned up my breakfast dishes, went into the den, and lackadaisically sank down on the sofa. It was Saturday morning, a time I usually love, and I didn't have anything I wanted to do. I picked up a magazine — one of many that my mother subscribes to — and idly glanced at the pictures of perfectly decorated rooms and beautiful, gourmet dishes.

Then my father walked into the den. "Morning, Liz," he said as he went to his desk and rummaged through some papers. "Manage to put off your Christmas shopping?"

"Yep," I answered.

"Me, too," he chuckled. "Maybe you and I will do some in the neighborhood later. It's less painful that way."

"Sure," I said.

He suddenly stopped whatever he was doing at his desk and looked at me. "How are the hands today?" he asked.

"Better," I said.

"Do you think you might give me a more than one-word response to my questions?"

"Much better," I said, and couldn't help smiling.

He sat down in the leather chair opposite me. "What's really bothering you?" he asked.

131

"Everything."

"I want at least a two-word response."

"Almost everything."

Then we both laughed, and I suddenly felt more like talking.

"It's weird," I said. "I was so excited yesterday because Tomo told me I could go all the way as a gymnast. He said I was Olympic material, and I should think it over, but that if I were serious about it I'd have to work out — every day and weekends."

"And that's what you want?"

"I thought so, but everything works against it. Yesterday I practiced so much on the bars, I ruined my hands. Tracy, who's been my best friend forever, didn't wait for me to walk home and she hasn't called. And mother — well, you know how she feels."

My father was silent for a while. Then he said, "Liz, I want you to come up into the attic with me."

"What on earth for? You going to stuff me in a trunk and ship me away?"

"Not exactly. I want to show you something."

"Okay," I said, slightly bewildered. "I didn't think there was anything to see up there but cobwebs and cartons."

"There are a few other items," he said mysteriously as he got up from his chair. I got up, too, and followed him as he trudged up the two flights of stairs to the attic. He flicked on the light switch and a bare bulb cast an eerie light over the suitcases and trunks that were stored under the eaves. He pulled out an old foot locker and knelt down to unfasten the clasps. Inside were some old army blankets, and I couldn't imagine what he dragged me upstairs to see. Then he stuck his hand under the folded blanket and pulled out a thin, maroon book.

"See this?" he said.

"Looks like a yearbook."

"That's exactly right." He flipped the pages until he came to a picture of the track team. "Look," he said, "do you recognize anyone?"

"Of course. That's you in the middle," I said, pointing to his picture. He was surrounded by members of the team in their track suits.

I read the caption and said, "I knew you were on the team, but I never knew you were the *captain*."

"I don't talk about it much," he said. Then he stuck his hand under the right-hand corner of the blanket and pulled out a small velvet box, which he carefully opened and held out for me to see.

"Wow!" I gasped. "That's beautiful." It was a gold medal with a runner engraved on it. He handed me the box so that I could examine it more carefully.

"You never told me about this," I said in amazement. "Why not?"

"It's not something I like to talk about. You see, it was the beginning and the end of something for me."

"What do you mean?"

"Let's get out of this dusty place and I'll tell you about it." He reached for the box I was holding, but I pulled away.

"Could I keep this in my room? I promise not to show it to anyone."

"Of course you can keep it. I just don't want it displayed."

"Okay," I said, not understanding why he felt so strongly.

Then he put back the yearbook, closed the lid, and shoved the foot locker into the corner.

I led the way downstairs, and stopped off at my room while my father watched in the doorway. "See," I said, as I pulled out my sweater drawer. "It'll be right here," and I pushed it in the corner under my sweaters.

We continued downstairs and into the den. I was dying of curiosity and couldn't help saying, "If that were my medal, I think I'd wear it on a chain around my neck."

My father chuckled as he sat down in the leather chair. "That's just what your mother wanted to do, but of course I wouldn't let her."

"You sound as though you're ashamed of it."

"That's not it," he said thoughtfully. "But in a strange way the medal represents a turning point in my life."

"What do you mean?"

"I mean I won that medal when I was a senior in high school at the county track meet. If someone had given me a million dollars, I couldn't have been more excited. It was the most exhilarating moment of my life."

"Did you go out for track at college?"

"I wanted to more than anything, but my family was very strapped for money. My father was a skilled laborer, and when he was laid off a job, he would get very depressed. I don't think he ever understood what that medal meant to me. His main concern was in me getting an education, so I'd have the credentials for a secure career."

"So you gave up track?"

"I felt I had no choice. I was lucky enough to get a science scholarship to Duke, and I couldn't risk losing it by taking time out for any extra-curricular activities."

"What does that have to do with me?"

"Nothing, really, except that I sometimes think what might have been if I hadn't listened to my father."

"You mean you might have entered the Olympics?"

"Who knows? My coach in high school thought I could make it."

"And your father discouraged you."

"It wasn't even considered. But Lizo, I don't think that should happen to you. I think it's better to make the attempt, and fail, than to go through life thinking what might have been."

"I want to make the attempt. And I know I have to decide for myself, not anyone else. That's what Tomo says."

"He's one hundred percent right."

"It's hard to fight everyone."

"You know I'm on your side."

"What about mother?"

"Don't worry. I can take care of her."

"That's all I wanted to hear. On Monday I'll tell Tomo that I'm ready to go."

# 22 _____

The next couple of weeks I learned what it meant to dedicate myself to something. Not only did I spend all my free time working out, but I had to be careful of what I ate. No more junk food, and lots of protein. Also, Tomo insisted I keep regular hours, including weekends. I couldn't consider spending an "overnight" at someone's house. Ellen and Jackie said they understood, but Tracy was still distant and I couldn't talk to her.

Carolyn came into my room one Sunday morning when I was still in bed. She wanted to borrow my ski sweater because she was going skating at the local rink. "You can come along," she said, "but I know you won't."

"Thanks, anyway. I'm going to the Y at noon."

"Even on Sunday?"

"I have a special pass. There's a security guard and the practice rooms are open, as well as the gym."

"You're destroying your social life, you know," she warned me.

"Can't help it," I said, wishing she'd lay off.

"And you'll never find a guy if you spend your weekends doing handsprings."

"My sweater is on the shelf in my closet," I said, and ducked my head under the pillow so she'd get the hint and shut up.

I heard her going into my closet and pull something down. I didn't come up for air until I was sure she was leaving the room. "Thanks," she said on her way out. "You're a good kid, even though you're crazy."

"Thanks a lot," I said, popping up in bed and fighting the twinge of suspicion that maybe she was right. My social life was suffering; maybe I wouldn't find a guy; I'd even had to turn down the Gardners, who had asked me to babysit. Maybe I was crazy, but I couldn't stop now. I was committed, but sometimes I felt very lonely.

As I walked to the Y, I couldn't stop thinking about what Carolyn had said. The empty streets made me feel more desolate than ever. But once I was inside the gym and started working on my floor routine I felt better. I practiced putting all my tricks together, trying to make them flow.

When I stopped for a few minutes to rest, I noticed someone else had slipped into the gym and was shooting baskets at the opposite end. He didn't seem to notice me and I went right on practicing. Then I went over to the high beam to work out. I had finally mastered my fear of the height, but I still took the precaution of dragging some extra mats over, just in case I should fall. I could do a number of stunts but I had to get them together so the routine would be smooth.

I was so intent on what I was doing that I didn't notice the basketball shooter had strolled over to watch me. I had just completed a backward roll, when I found him staring at me. It was Roger Kimball. Suddenly I felt very self-conscious and stopped cold. I sat on the beam, my legs dangling.

"Don't stop," he said. "You're really good."

"Just resting," I told him, which was half true.

"What're you doing here on a Sunday? Practicing for the Olympics?"

"How d'ja guess?" I said smiling. "What're *you* doing here? I thought I was the only crazy one."

"I'm glad there're two of us. Maybe we'll go crazy together," he joked.

"What are you training for?"

"Really, I'm practicing my foul shots. Since I'm the shortest member of the basketball team, I'm constantly getting fouled by the opponents. That means I'm entitled to a lot of free throws, and I'm trying to perfect them."

"You don't look so short to me," I said, appraising him from his sneakers to the top of his curly brown hair.

"Five-nine doesn't make me a midget, but almost everyone else is six feet or over."

"I get it. I didn't know you were on the basketball team. All I know is you write awfully good editorials."

He looked startled, but recovered enough to say, "Am I famous?"

"I guess so. You're a year ahead of me, and since you're the associate editor on the newspaper, everyone knows who you are."

"That's amazing," he said, looking pleased. "I'd really like to be known for my basketball playing, though. You can understand that, seeing as you're so serious about gymnastics. Last time I saw you it was your first day."

"I *am* serious," I said.

"You wouldn't be here if you weren't. You've turned what I consider a boring practice session practically into a party. I've had enough of free shooting, so do you mind if I watch you for a while?"

"Sure, if you want to. In fact, now I can practice on the uneven bars. Tomo doesn't want me to work on the bars alone."

"I'd love to catch you if you fall."

I could feel myself blushing and didn't know what to say, so I jumped off the beam and headed for the bars.

"This way," I said.

My palms had toughened up but I was careful to chalk my hands so I wouldn't stick to the bar. I went through my routine, including the Mill Circle Catch, which for the first time went well.

Roger was impressed, and sounded almost surprised when he said, "That's terrific."

"That's the best it's ever gone."

"Maybe I should be your weekend coach."

"Maybe."

"How much longer are you staying?"

"At least an hour. It's not worth the trip, otherwise."

"You *are* serious, aren't you?"

"What's wrong with that?" I asked defensively, and what Carolyn had said that morning flashed through my mind. *You'll never find a guy if you spend your weekends doing handsprings.*

"Nothing's wrong. I think it's great."

"Honestly?"

"Honestly. You sound surprised."

"That's because almost everyone is giving me a hard time — except my father. He understands."

"He probably was a competitive athlete."

"That's right," I said in amazement. "How did you know?"

"Because only people who have been through it understand what has to happen."

"Have you been through it?"

"In a way. I don't really have the natural ability, but I love basketball and I was determined to make the team. Because of my size, I had to work ten times harder than anyone else."

"And you made it, right?"

"Right, and now I'm still working harder than anyone else. Like Alice in Wonderland, I have to run twice as fast just to stay in place."

"You do understand," I said thoughtfully. "But sometimes I wonder if it's worth it."

"Why wouldn't it be?"

"I get a lot of flak from my mother and sister, and even my best friend is turned off."

"It's worth it, Liz," he said seriously. "I'm taking up your precious time. You didn't come here to talk. Why don't I shoot some more baskets, and you practice some more, and then I'll walk you home."

"Good idea," I said, grasping the bar and doing a Back Hip Circle.

"You *are* good," Roger said, appraising me.

"Thanks," I said, as he backed away, still watching me.

Wait till I tell Carolyn, I thought, as I skipped over to the mats to work on my floor routine. Then I mused, Maybe Carolyn's right, it's time I learned how to apply some makeup.

# 23

In keeping with my roller coaster theory of life, I seemed to be heading for a smoother ride. Roger not only walked me home from the Y that Sunday, but invited me to the movies for the following Friday. He understood perfectly about my training and never pushed me into breaking my schedule.

I think Carolyn was amazed and impressed that Roger paid so much attention to me. She said everyone in the senior class knew who he was because of his position on the paper, and that next year he was definitely slated to be editor-in-chief.

"I didn't know he was a jock besides," she said.

"And not a dumb one, either," I pointed out.

"That's for sure," she agreed.

It seemed to me that both Carolyn and E.J. saw me in a new light. Or maybe it was *me* seeing myself differently. At any rate, I no longer felt like some kind of freak around the house, and whenever I wavered or felt I was missing out on something, Roger told me, "It's worth it."

Then another amazing thing happened, and for the first time *I* felt like the older sister. It was the night after the school play, *Cabaret*. Ellen, Tracy, Jackie, and I sat together and afterward there was a party in the gym.

Roger wanted me to meet him there, but I told him it was too close to the competition for me to bend my rules. He didn't press me and instead insisted on walking me home. Then he had to go back to the party because he was doing a a feature story on the evening and had to interview members of the cast as well as people in the audience.

I was getting ready for bed when I heard someone shuffling up the stairs. I stuck my head out my door and was surprised to see it was Carolyn. "What did you forget?" I asked, knowing *she* would never leave a party early.

Then I noticed her eyes were red and puffy and she was sniffling. For a minute I thought she must be getting a virus, but she actually started sobbing, and went into her room. She didn't slam the door, so I followed her. She grabbed a tissue from the container on her dressing table and collapsed on her daybed.

"Are you all right?" I asked genuinely concerned.

"No, I'm terrible," she answered in between blowing her nose and blotting her tears.

"What's wrong?"

"Steve is what's wrong," she said angrily. "Not

only did he not ask me to go to the play with him, but afterward at the party he acted as though I wasn't even there."

"Maybe he didn't see you."

"He saw me, all right. He said hello as he brushed by me on the way to the punch bowl, but he didn't even stop to talk. The rest of the time he just ignored me."

"And that's why you came home?"

"The whole scene was a real bummer and I didn't think I could cope, so I just slipped out. Nobody's going to miss me," she said miserably. She started sobbing worse than ever. I sat down at her dressing table and tossed her some more tissues.

"He's not the last guy in the world. Besides, you've got a million others calling all the time."

"But he's the only one I care about. Don't you understand?"

"Guess so."

"Listen, you don't know how lucky you are that you've got gymnastics. I know I've always teased you about it, but right now I'd give anything to be turned on by something besides men."

"You probably will someday. It'll just hit you like it did me."

"And not only that, you've got Roger. I even know some seniors who think he's cute."

"He is sort of a fringe benefit."

"That's all?" she said knowingly, and for the first time she actually stopped crying and was half-smiling.

We both laughed, and Carolyn didn't seem quite so unhappy. "Now, in keeping with your schedule, it's time for you to go to sleep," she said in her usual older-sister manner.

"And what about you?"

"I'll drown my problems in the bathtub."

"You'll feel fine tomorrow, I know it. But you've got to start going out with other guys. That's the best way to recover."

"I know you're right. And for all your good advice, I think I'll give you a makeup lesson tomorrow. We'll start with blush-on and lip gloss."

"I'm ready," I said.

"You'll be the most glamorous gymnast in the competition."

"That's not why I'm doing it."

"It's not?" she asked innocently.

I smiled sheepishly and Carolyn said, "Oh, yeah, for a minute I forgot about the fringe benefit."

"Good night," I said, and stood up, unable to think of any adequate response.

"Good night. Did you know that the hours you sleep before midnight are considered 'beauty sleep'?"

"That's not why I'm doing it," I said again, seriously. Then I realized that Carolyn was kidding me. But since it was about Roger, I didn't mind at all.

I was looking forward to my makeup lesson the following morning, but it was ten o'clock and Carolyn still wasn't up. I was hoping to get my new face before Roger met me. We were going to the coffee shop for a sandwich before I went on to the Y, so all I was having was tea for breakfast.

Fortunately the phone rang, and since it was some boy calling for Carolyn I had a legitimate reason to shout upstairs and wake her up. When she came downstairs a few minutes later, she seemed in a lot better mood that the night before.

"Men are all crazy," she said smiling to herself, and grabbed a banana. Then she looked at me. "Hey, didn't I promise you a lesson?"

"Yep."

"Better hurry. I have a lunch date in the city."

"Somebody new, I bet."

"How d'ja guess?"

"Never mind,"I said. At that point I was more interested in my own love life than in hers. "I have a lunch date, too, you know."

"Well, then, let's get started," she said and threw the banana peel in the garbage pail. I put my tea cup in the sink and followed her upstairs into her room.

"Sit," she ordered, pointing to the bench in front of her vanity table. She pulled up a chair and turned on the makeup mirror.

For the first time I actually examined all the cosmetics which Carolyn had acquired. There were a zillion jars filled with what looked like pink paste. One cup had nothing but different sized brushes. There were mascara pots, eyebrow pencils, tweezers, and assorted powders. I must have looked alarmed because Carolyn said laughing, "Don't be scared."

"That looks like a witches' brew."

"I promise not to do anything too dramatic. You're the natural type."

"I'm in your hands," I said, wondering what I'd gotten myself into.

"What are you wearing today?" Carolyn asked.

"What difference does that make?"

"It makes a lot of difference, dummy. If you wear a red sweater you shouldn't wear brown eye shadow."

"I never thought of that, but it makes sense."

"What are you wearing?" she repeated.

"My green sweater."

"Good. I have the perfect eye shadow. It's called Quiet Sea." She pulled out a small case and ordered me to close my eyes. Then she proceeded to apply some pale green stuff to my lids. When she finished, she leaned back and said, "Perfect."

I stared at myself in the mirror and I really was pleased with the result.

"Now watch, I'll show you how to put on blush." She took a brush and spread color over her cheeks. "Now you do it."

I imitated her, and decided the results weren't bad at all.

"Now add some lip gloss," she commanded.

"Great for chapped lips," I observed, as I rubbed it on.

"You would think of that."

Then we both stared at my image in the mirror.

"Definitely an improvement," Carolyn observed.

"Thanks a lot," I groaned.

"Actually, you look smashing."

"You mean it?"

"I mean it. Now go, otherwise I'll be late and it'll be all your fault. And have fun."

"You too," I said, "and thanks."

I ran out of her room and got dressed, carefully pulling my green sweater over my head. I wanted to preserve my face at least until I met Roger.

I knew I'd be early, but I didn't feel like waiting around, so I slowly walked to the coffee shop. To my amazement, Roger was already there, sitting at the fountain. We both looked surprised.

"I didn't know you were famous for your promptness," I said, as I sat down next to him.

"I'm not," he answered. "I just didn't feel like hanging around the house."

"Me neither," I admitted.

"It's too early for lunch. Let's go for a walk."

"Good idea."

"We'll be back," Roger said to the gawky-looking boy who was behind the counter. The kid shrugged his shoulders as though we were crazy, and Roger and I both tried not to laugh till we walked out the door. When we got outside, I had a case of the giggles, and Roger said, "Pull yourself together."

"He must think we've gone bananas."

"We have," Roger said, and reached for my hand. "You better hang on to me for support."

I started walking, but Roger remained in one spot, staring at me while I was tugging at his hand. "Hey," he said, "wait a minute."

"What's wrong?" I asked.

"You look different."

"I do," I said, evenly.

"Different is not the word. You look terrific."

"Thanks," I said, feeling very self-conscious.

"In fact, you're prettier than ever."

"C'mon," I said, "I thought we were going for a walk."

"We are, but can't I look at you for a while?"

"Roger," I wailed, "do you want everyone in the world to think we're crazy?"

"I really don't care," he said smiling. "But if you insist on walking, let's go," and he gently squeezed my hand as we started to stroll around the block.

We didn't say anything for a while, but a million thoughts were racing through my head. One thing I wondered was how Carolyn would handle a compliment. But I already knew the answer. If anyone told her she looked "prettier than ever," she wouldn't be fazed at all — she'd simply say "thank you." I hoped I'd have another chance to use that response!

# 24

Finally, school was out for Christmas vacation. It was a relief not to have to worry about homework for a change. I'd been doing most of mine during study hall, a time when Tracy and I used to send notes back and forth and try to suppress the giggles.

Now since I didn't have time after school and was too tired at night, study hall was the only time I got any homework done. Of course that meant, according to Tracy, that I wasn't any fun anymore. And I suppose I wasn't, but Tracy seemed to me to be totally lacking in understanding.

Although school was closed, naturally, for the holidays, the Y remained open, and Tomo continued to have classes. I still worked out daily, and it was beginning to pay off. I had reached a new plateau and Tomo kept encouraging me to learn new tricks. I was really thrilled when I could do a front aerial and a flip flop. Tomo said my progress was amazing.

It was the day after Christmas, and our regular class met. Tomo asked me to show the class my tumbling routine, and when I did my aerials there was a collective gasp. When I finished, everyone applauded and a lot of the girls came over to compliment me. Tracy, however, seemed very busy talking to someone and didn't say anything to me. I tried not to worry about that, and when Jeanne tugged my arm and said, "Let's work on the horse," I gladly followed her.

We took turns ricocheting off the board, and I concentrated hard on my landing, knowing that my body should be in balance with good posture and that I shouldn't take any steps when the vault is completed.

Jeanne had just finished her third turn when there was a commotion at the opposite end of the gym. A group was huddled around someone, and I was shocked to see it was Tracy. Jeanne and I went running over to where Tracy was now sitting on the floor, grasping her ankle. Tomo was kneeling beside her.

"What happened?" I asked alarmed.

"It's nothing," Tracy answered. She wasn't crying, but her face looked very white. "I was doing a round-off flip flop and my ankle twisted."

"Do you want me to take you home?" I asked.

"No, thanks," she said evenly. "Ginger's gone to call my mother. I'm pretty sure she's home now and she'll pick me up."

"I need a strong girl," Tomo said, looking up at the group that had gathered around. "You, Peggy. Let's make a seat, and we'll carry Tracy into the supervisor's office. Then we'll dampen a towel in some ice water and wrap her ankle."

Ginger then came running back, saying she had reached Tracy's mother, who would be over right away. "Comes in handy having a nurse for a mother," she added.

"You sure you don't want me to wait with you?" I asked Tracy as Tomo helped her up. She stood on one foot while he and Peggy, a senior who was a horsy-looking girl, formed a seat for her with their arms. Then Tracy seated herself on their crossed arms, and snapped at me, "I wouldn't want you to miss any precious practice time."

I don't know if anyone else noticed, but I was speechless at Tracy's reaction.

"I'll be right back," Tomo said as he moved toward the door, carrying Tracy with Peggy. "Take a five-minute break."

I was still standing in one spot, stunned, when Jeanne came up to me. "It's her problem," she said softly, "and you shouldn't be so upset."

"She *was* my best friend. I guess I'll just have to get used to that."

"Maybe she still will be," Jeanne said. "Now that she's out of the running, she doesn't have to compete with you. In fact, that's probably why she did it."

"What're you talking about?" I asked, baffled. We had strolled to the far side of the gym away from everyone, and were leaning against the wall.

"Some people think there's no such thing as

an 'accident.' And Tracy busting her ankle —
or whatever she did to it — could have been done
on purpose."

"That seems like a painful way to get out of
something."

"She didn't do it on a conscious level."

"You always have these complicated explanations for things, but somehow you make a lot of
sense."

"That's what my brother says," Jeanne said
proudly. "That's why he says I should be a psychologist."

"You already are," I told her.

Then Tomo and Peggy reappeared. "Tracy's
mother is on her way and Mrs. Oliver is waiting
with Tracy," Tomo announced. "Now, we've got
a half hour left. Let's go back to work."

I practiced hard for the rest of the period, trying not to think about Tracy. I knew Jeanne was
right; it was Tracy's problem, but it's hard to lose
a best friend, especially if it's not your fault.

I decided not to talk about my relationship
with Tracy when I got home, but I knew I would
have to tell my mother and Carolyn about her
mishap. They would find out anyway, and it
would be weird if they didn't hear it from me.
I didn't want to blow it up out of proportion
because then E.J. might overreact and go hysteri-
cal like she did about my bleeding hands.

When I got home E.J. was scraping carrots
over the sink, and when she saw me she immediately stopped what she was doing, wiped her
hands on her apron, and said, "Come here, you."

I walked over to her and she put her hands on my shoulders and planted a kiss on my forehead. I was a little bewildered because E.J. rarely gives me such an effusive hello.

"Elizabeth, I just want you to know that two of my bridge club ladies, Norma Jean and Phyllis, say that your reputation as a gymnast is fabulous. Phyllis's niece, Peggy, whom Phyllis describes as a horse, won't even be entering the local competition. Phyllis says she can't believe that such a delicate little thing like you could be such a superb athlete."

"Gee, thanks," I said, beaming.

"And Norma Jean says the word is out that you'll probably be the best in the school — maybe even in the county."

"How about the country?" I asked, unable to stop smiling.

"Oh, I wouldn't be surprised at anything now. Honey, I am so proud of you. Now go take a shower so your muscles don't cramp up."

"Mother, you'd be a great coach," I said as I floated up the stairs.

As I stood in the shower, I couldn't believe how E.J. had come around. But that wasn't the end of my surprises. When I finished showering, changed my clothes, and went back downstairs, I said to E.J., who was basting a roast chicken, "Tracy did something to her ankle today in gymnastics. She had to go home early and she'll probably be out of it for a while."

At that moment, my father stuck his head in doorway from the dining room. My mother didn't notice him, she was so intent on her basting. Then she turned to me and said seriously, "I suppose those things happen. Just one of the risks of being an athlete."

I looked at my father, who still hadn't said anything. He covered his mouth with his hand, trying not to laugh, and gave me a slow wink.

# 25 ───────────

It was the day before New Year's Eve and I had faithfully worked out daily at the Y. Now that my whole family was so encouraging, it was a lot easier to keep to my schedule. Roger often met me at the Y so he could shoot baskets, and then we'd stop for a hamburger and he would walk me home.

New Year's Eve, Jackie was having a bunch of kids over and naturally I invited Roger who had already made me promise that I'd go with him that night. That was one promise I wouldn't find hard to keep! It was going to be the one night of the year that I wouldn't be asleep by eleven. Even Tomo said I was entitled to break training once.

I still had this nagging concern about Tracy and me. All these good things were happening, and I couldn't tell her about them, and I wasn't so sure now that she'd want to hear them. I had heard that her ankle wasn't broken but that she had pulled a ligament and was supposed to stay off her leg. I really wanted to visit her and maybe cheer her up, but I was afraid of how she'd react.

I finally confided my dilemma to Jeanne, explaining that things were going so well in my life, and obviously they weren't exactly terrific for Tracy.

"You can afford to be generous then," Jeanne said that evening when I called for advice.

"What does that mean?"

"It means that it's bothering you that you haven't seen her, so you might just as well. You have nothing to lose, except maybe a few awkward moments. Call first, and if she doesn't want to see you you'll get the vibes immediately."

"You make it sound so simple. But I think you're right. I'm going to call right now."

"Good luck. And let me know what happens."

"You'll be the first. Bye now." I hung up and sat by the phone in the kitchen, my hand still on the receiver, and took a deep breath. Then I dialed Tracy's phone number and after three rings her mother answered. She sounded surprised to hear my voice. "Where've you been? I was sure you'd have come over by now."

"I'd like to, tomorrow," I said quickly, aware that Tracy hadn't told her anything.

"Well, I'm sure Tracy would love to see you. She's resting now and I don't want to get her out of bed. She's supposed to keep her leg elevated, and I've had trouble keeping her down. What time do you think you'll get here?"

"I'll be there around one."

"Plan to have lunch."

"Thanks a lot. But don't you think you should ask Tracy first?"

"Don't be ridiculous. You'll be the perfect tonic for her. She's not having any fun this vacation, and you'll cheer her up."

"I'll do my best," I said hesitantly, and hung up, feeling more guilt than anger now. But that night I went to bed and was relieved to know that I'd taken a positive step and that whatever was going on with me and Tracy would be resolved the next day.

The following morning I worked out at the Y and then went directly to Tracy's apartment. On the way, I stopped at the local florist and picked up a little cactus that was planted in a ceramic pink elephant. It seemed perfect for New Year's Eve and I hoped Tracy would like it as much as I did, but I wasn't counting on it.

When I got to Tracy's, her mother answered the door and said she'd prepared some tuna sandwiches and homemade brownies, and there were Cokes in the fridge. "Help yourself to anything. And now that you're here, I'm going out for a while. I have to pick up a few things. Tracy's in bed watching television."

"Take your time," I said.

"What's that you're holding?" she asked, looking at the plant.

"It's for Tracy. A cactus in a pink elephant."

"Sounds adorable, but I won't spoil the wrapping. You are a good friend," she said as she took her coat from the hall closet.

I gulped and said, "See ya later."

I walked into Tracy's room, where she was on top of the covers in her pajamas, her leg on a stack of pillows. She was watching some game show on the tube.

"Hi ya," I said, tentatively.

"Hi ya," she said, and snapped off the TV with a remote control switch.

"Anything good on?" I asked.

"Borrrrring," she said.

"Here," I said. "This might cheer you up." I handed her the plant.

She unwrapped it, half-smiled, and then burst into tears.

"That's a funny reaction," I said, totally confused. "Are you all right? You look okay."

"On the outside, maybe. Inside, I'm a mess." The tears were streaming down her face, and she clutched a bunch of tissues that were on her night table.

"What are you talking about? The pink elephant is supposed to make you happy."

"I don't deserve it," she sobbed. "I'm surprised you're even speaking to me, I've been so awful."

"Well, I thought something was bugging you," I admitted. "But I wasn't sure what. And frankly, you weren't too approachable." I dumped my parka and sank into the chair at the side of her bed.

"I guess there was a lot bugging me," she said, still sniffling. "And I suppose if we still believed in that Truth Table, I could tell all."

"Maybe it's not such a dumb idea to tell all, anyway. I'm still your friend, you know."

With that, she cried harder than ever. Then

she stopped suddenly and said, "You're right. It's not such a dumb idea. I've had plently of time to think these past few days, and I know I haven't been in a really terrific mood for ages."

"I'll agree with that," I said mildly, feeling that this was the first time in weeks that Tracy had sounded like her old self. "Maybe you should figure out why."

"That's exactly what I'm going to do. I guess one of the reasons it's taken me so long is because everything was gradual . . . I mean I was gradually feeling deserted."

"By whom?"

"First by my mother. She really is serious about Dr. Friedman, and it's not that I'm not happy for her, but in the meantime I don't think she needs me anymore."

"That's crazy."

"I know it is, and he's really nice to me. Anyhow, one thing I've figured out lying here in my bed of pain is that it's really better for both of us if she has someone besides me to think about. She used to ask me a lot of details about school and stuff, and I kind of resented it. Now, I almost miss it. Do you think that's crazy?"

"Perfectly normal adolescent behavior," I said in my parental voice, and for the first time Tracy actually laughed out loud.

"What else have you figured out?" I asked, knowing I was digging for her to reveal some truth about us.

"Well, it's stupid, but I guess I resented you because I talked you into taking gymnastics, and before I knew it, you were better than me — in fact, you're by far the best in the class. Tomo recognized it right away. I just couldn't face it, until I put myself out of commission and had a chance to think. I practically broke my neck in the process."

"You mean you twisted your ankle on purpose?" I asked, remembering Jeanne's theory.

"Of course not. But it did give me an opportunity to see things as they really are, instead of the way I hoped they would be."

"That's really big of you to admit. I guess I've been kind of a pill about practicing. It's just that it means so much to me."

"I know it does. And you really are a good friend to have put up with me and my downers."

"What're friends for?" I asked idiotically.

"Right now, I'd say they're for getting some tuna sandwiches and Cokes in here," Tracy said in her old good-humored way.

"Coming right up," I said, leaping out of my chair, and thinking that I'd never before been so happy to wait on someone.

## 26

We were talking non-stop for about an hour. It was as though a dam had burst and all our pent-up emotions had been released. When Tracy's mother returned and looked in on us she said to me, "I didn't need my nurse's training to tell me you're exactly what the doctor ordered. Tracy actually looks better since you're here."

"Then I can go to Jackie's," Tracy exclaimed.

"Do you feel up to it?" her mother asked.

"Now I do. I have to practice using my crutches, though."

"You mean you weren't planning to go to the party?" I asked, surprised that Tracy would ever miss a get-together.

"To tell the truth," Tracy said, "I wasn't in the mood for a party. I guess I was feeling a little like a martyr, although for the life of me I couldn't tell what I was sacrificing myself for."

"I hope it's not an all-night party," Mrs. Nearing said.

"Don't worry," I told her. "I promised myself I'll be home by one. My father is going to pick me up and we can drop Tracy home."

"That would be wonderful. You really are the best friend!"

"You're not kidding," Tracy said.

I was getting embarrassed and was happy when Tracy's mother noticed the cactus. "That's the cutest thing. And when the cactus goes, you can use the elephant for a pencil holder."

"I have to go," I told Tracy. "You've got to practice walking on three feet, and I've got to go home and take a hot bath. Otherwise, I won't be able to move."

"I'll see you, Liz. And thanks for everything. I feel one hundred percent better. Even my ankle's stopped hurting."

"That's great," I said.

"You could hang out a shingle and get paid for services rendered."

"That's an idea, but I wouldn't know how much to charge."

"That's good, because I could never repay you."

"You already have," I said as I headed for the door.

"Later," Tracy said to my back.

"Later," I said, without turning.

I don't know how I got home but I felt that a great weight had been lifted. In a few hours it would be the New Year. As I approached our house I knocked wood on the tree next to the path that led to the front door.

This was the last day of the year, and the happiest day of my life. I didn't think things could ever get better.

# 27 ⎯⎯⎯⎯⎯⎯⎯

The party at Jackie's was the greatest. Actually, it was like a lot of parties, with punch and disco dancing, and loads of junk food. I figured out that that night I would have had a terrific time even if we'd been put in an empty room with no food or drinks or music — only our imaginations.

Tracy had a ball because even though she couldn't dance, everyone paid a lot of attention to her. She was constantly surrounded, and enjoyed holding court.

At one point I cornered Jeanne and said, "Mission accomplished."

"I could tell," she said smiling.

"Thanks to you, I did the right thing."

"It was obvious."

"To you, maybe, but I needed the push."

Then Arthur, the class clown, made the lights flicker and announced, "Five minutes till the New Year. Be prepared!"

Roger moved over to me, and then the lights went out completely. He put his arm around my shoulder and said, "Are you prepared?"

"What for?"

"For this," he said, and pulled me toward him. The TV cast the only light in the room. The screen showed the dropping ball at Times Square, and then the announcer appeared and shouted, "Happy New Year, everyone!"

"Happy New Year, Liz. I never thought basketball would be responsible for my love life."

"Happy New Year, Roge. I never thought gymnastics would lead to this, either."

Then he kissed me, and Arthur, who is not known for his timing, turned on the lights. A lot of couples stayed in a huddle, but I was too self-conscious. It was all over very fast, but I would remember that kiss for a long time.

There was only an hour left until I turned into a pumpkin, and it didn't seem fair that time couldn't freeze for a while. I didn't want to leave the party, and I said to Roger, "Maybe I should call my father and tell him not to come over till two. He won't care because my parents are entertaining at home and they always stay up late New Year's Eve."

"No way," Roger said adamantly. "It's bad enough that you're staying up past your usual curfew."

"But I'm having such a good time."

"That's beside the point. You're in training, remember?"

"I remember. But is it worth it?"

"I've told you a million times, yes, it's worth it."

"You're right," I admitted reluctantly.

"I know I'm right. Besides, you've got less than three weeks to go. You don't want to blow it because of one party."

"Guess not," I said petulantly.

"Are you serious about being an athlete or not?" Roger asked, slightly annoyed.

"I'm serious," I answered, and suddenly realized how lucky I was to have someone like Roger who really cared, but I couldn't come out and tell him so. Instead, I put the blame on him. "It's your fault, you know."

"What's my fault?"

"That I want to stay at the party. I've honestly never had such a good time."

Roger didn't seem annoyed anymore, and a huge smile spread over his face. "I am flattered, Liz, but you'd never forgive me for letting you get exhausted. And there'll be a lot more parties in your life."

"And not a lot more competitions if I don't do well in this one."

"Exactly."

"I'd better collect Tracy, and get our coats. I don't want to keep my father waiting."

"Maybe he'll drop me off, too."

"You don't have to leave yet," I said, surprised that he would even consider the idea.

"Don't be silly, Liz. As far as I'm concerned, it won't be a party if you're not here."

"You mean it, don't you?"

"Absolutely." He glanced at his watch. "We've got twenty minutes til countdown — time for some more dancing."

Roger grabbed my hand and pulled me onto the floor at the end of the living room where one of the throw rugs had been pulled up.

"This is the best New Year's Eve I've ever had," Roger whispered in my ear, holding me close.

"Me, too," I said, thinking that for the first time in my life I could understand where Carolyn's head was at when it came to men. She'd always kidded me about being a late bloomer. One thing was for sure, after tonight I'd be well on my way to catching up with her!

# 28_____

The next three weeks melded together, and I was scared and excited at the same time as the day of the competition approached. Now that Tracy was incapacitated, it was only me and Jeanne who would be entering from Tomo's class in the fifteen-and-up group.

The school paper did a feature story on me and Jeanne, and even took pictures. We both were interviewed by the sports editor and by Roger. Jeanne said she loved gymnastics and was looking forward to the competition, but the one to watch was Elizabeth Franklin. I thought that was really generous of her, and I know she didn't mean to, but in a way what she said made me feel that a lot of people from my school were counting on me to do well.

The night before the competition I could hardly eat. E.J. kept saying, "Don't be upset. Everyone says you'll do just fine."

What she didn't understand was that I wanted to do more than "just fine." I wanted to be perfect so that I would know I could enter the sectional in March and the state competition in April.

Carolyn tried to understand my feelings but she wasn't much better than E.J. "You've worked really hard," she said, "and it's not as though this is the last local competition. There's another in February, and you'll get another crack at it then."

"That's true," I said, but I didn't feel too comforted by that prospect.

My father understood best of all, and while I was trying to choke down some chicken, he told me, "You've done everything possible to train for tomorrow, and that's all anyone can expect of you, including yourself. You don't have to be a perfect girl. Don't give yourself a hard time. No matter what happens, you'll have the satisfaction of knowing you've tried your best, and nobody can take that away from you."

I nodded my head and pushed my plate away.

"You need your strength," E.J. scolded. "Can't you eat a little more?"

"Not without throwing up," I answered, and for the first time that evening I actually smiled, everyone else laughed, and the world didn't seem so deadly serious.

After I helped clean up the kitchen I tried watching television in the den. Even though my favorite program, *Family*, was on, I couldn't concentrate on it. My father noticed how restless I was and suggested I drink a cup of hot cocoa made with milk. "Milk is guaranteed to make you sleep," he said.

"I'll try anything. The way I feel now, I'll be up all night."

As soon as the program was over, I fixed the cocoa. Then Roger called to wish me luck. He could tell I was jumpy and said, "Instead of thinking about tomorrow, think about New Year's Eve — midnight to be exact."

"Good idea," I said.

After Roger called, I went upstairs to get ready for bed. I took a hot bath and then, without knowing why, before I climbed into bed I fumbled in my sweater drawer and took out the velvet box containing my father's gold medal. I'm not superstitious, but I couldn't resist removing the medal from its box and putting it under my pillow. Maybe, subconsciously, I thought it would bring me good luck.

At ten o'clock I turned out my light and started reviewing in my mind my routines, and then I tried to concentrate on Roger, and then I repeated to myself, like a litany, what my father had said. *You've done everything possible to train for tomorrow, and that's all anyone can expect of you, including yourself. You don't have to be perfect.* Eventually, miraculously, I fell asleep, and didn't wake up until seven o'clock. I was glad it was that late, but I still had two hours to kill before I was expected at the Y.

I carefully made my bed, returned the gold medal to its box in my drawer, put on my lavender leotard that Jeanne and Tracy and I had originally decided would be distinctive-looking without being flashy, and went downstairs. I went through the motions of putting cornflakes in a bowl with milk and sugar. I was dawdling over my cereal at the kitchen table when my father appeared.

"Morning, Liz," he said, as he put water into the kettle for coffee. "How long until countdown?"

"I have to be at the Y at nine o'clock for warm-up and to get instructions and stuff. The meet doesn't officially begin until ten."

"Do you want me to drive you over? I can come back and pick up mother and Carolyn."

"No, thanks. I think I'd rather walk. It'll kill time, and it's a beautiful day."

"You're probably right."

Then E.J. came into the kitchen, wearing her robe and slippers. I can always tell when my mother is nervous, because she asks a lot of questions and doesn't wait for answers. "Elizabeth, honey," she began, "would you like some eggs? I'm going to make a batch of scrambled and maybe you'll have some. How are you getting to the Y? I know you have to be there before we do. We can all drive you over. I understand we're lucky that the Y is big enough to have four events going on at once. People from all over the county are going to participate, and Phyllis says they expect the bleachers will be filled with spectators. She says the entire school is coming out to watch."

My father started chuckling, and said, "Take it easy. If you keep this up, you'll get us all upset."

"Who's upset?" E.J. asked, and abruptly stopped mixing the eggs. E.J. realized she'd been babbling, and broke into smiles.

"You're right," she said, "I am carrying on, but I'm so excited."

"We all are," my father said.

"I think it's time for me to get going," I said.

Carolyn came into the kitchen just as I was getting up from my chair.

"Today's the day. I'm keeping my fingers crossed for you," she said as she held up her hands and waved her crossed fingers in the air.

"Thanks," I said.

Then E.J. put down her mixing spoon and put her arms around me. "Good luck, honey. I know you'll do great."

"Next," my father said, as she moved out of the way. "Good luck, Lizo." He gave me a quick hug.

"Thanks, everyone," I said. "Now I've really got to go." I got out of there fast, wanting to escape all the emotion. I had put my jeans and a shirt over my leotard, so all I did was grab my parka and hurry out.

It was good to be out of the house, and the brief walk to the Y had a calming effect on my nerves. I went directly downstairs to the locker room to leave my clothes, and by the time I got upstairs to the gym, a lot of strange people were milling around. The calming effect of my walk was fading rapidly.

Tomo was talking to Jeanne at the opposite end of the gym and I ran over to them. "Hi ya," I said breathlessly. "I'm not late, am I?"

"Hi ya," Jeanne said.

"You're right on time. I'm just about to open our packet of information," Tomo said as he ripped open an envelope.

"Where are our numbers?" Jeanne asked.

"Right here." Tomo withdrew two cloth numbers and then looked at a mimeographed sheet of paper. "Jeanne, you're number 22, and Liz, you're 18."

"How do we attach them?" I asked worriedly.

"Fortunately, I've had experience in these matters," Tomo said, and with a flourish pulled a needle and roll of thread out of his pocket. "Courtesy of Mrs. Oliver. She always keeps sewing supplies in her desk and I remembered to bring them to the gym. You can tack them on each others back."

"I'll do you first," Jeanne volunteered.

"Just don't stick me," I pleaded, turning my back to her.

"Don't worry."

"While you're getting sewed, can you listen at the same time?" Tomo asked.

"Sure," Jeanne said.

"I'll try," I said.

"That's the most I can ask," Tomo said smiling. If he was nervous, he sure didn't show it.

Then he proceeded to tell us the information on the mimeographed sheet. "There are forty entries, and there will be four events going on at the same time. That's one of the reasons we were lucky enough to have *our* Y chosen for the site of the competition. Many gyms can't accommodate four events at once."

"Wait a minute. You're all sewed up, Liz."

"Thanks. Now I'll do you." She handed me the needle and thread and I started to thread the needle but my hands were shaking too much.

"I'll do that," Jeanne said, and I gratefully handed the needle and thread to her. She seemed really cool and that helped steady my nerves so that I was able to tack her number on her back without stabbing her.

Tomo went on, "A score of ten for each event is perfect. There are four judges, and a head judge for each event. The head averages the final score."

"How?" Jeanne asked.

"The high score and the low score are dropped, and the average of the middle scores determines the final score."

"Then what?" I wanted to know.

"A runner takes the score to the scoring table, and it is flashed on a pole."

"That thing down there?" I asked, pointing to a pole that looked like a T bar at the far end of the gym where there was a table and some people who were obviously officials talking.

"That's right. The pole is slowly turned after

each performance so that everyone can see the results.''

I felt my insides do a flip flop when he said that. What if I froze at the bars or overshot the beam or tripped on the vault or lost my way in the floor routine. *Don't give yourself a hard time*, I could hear my father saying, and I tried to stay cool.

The bleachers were getting filled and I was almost relieved when the official sitting at the scoring table announced in a deep voice that the warm-up would begin. Before I took my position on the floor I searched the bleachers for my friends and family. I noticed my mother sitting with her bridge friends in the middle row. Tracy was easy to see because she was sitting holding her crutches in the front row. Ellen and Jackie were next to her. Carolyn was seated between two boys with a bunch of kids from her class. I had a moment of panic because I couldn't find my father. I guess I must have showed it on my face, because Jeanne, who had just finished waving to her mother, looked at me and said, "What's wrong?"

"I can't find my father."

"He's right there," Jeanne said, and pointed to where he was sitting midway up the bleachers, but off to one side, by himself. I was relieved to see him and thought to myself that more than anyone he knew what I was going through.

Then I spotted Roger, who was sitting down front with the school newspaper staff. I resisted waving to him because Tomo had warned us that paying attention to the audience would lessen our concentration. It was hard advice to follow.

Jeanne was having the same problem and couldn't resist whispering to me that even Mr. Vargas, the principal, was in the bleachers on the top row. I looked up and saw him surrounded by other teachers, and then I even saw the Gardners with Miriam. It flashed through my mind that everyone I knew in the entire world was here, watching me.

The deep-voiced official sitting at the scoring table announced: "Take your places for the first fifteen-minute warm-up rotation."

It was a relief to start doing the warm-up exercises. Then, after what seemed more like fifteen seconds than fifteen minutes, the official ordered: "Clear the floor, please. The competition will begin."

The first event for me was the floor. I was the fourth in line and waiting for my turn wasn't easy. I thought so hard about my routine I hardly noticed what the others were doing. Then I heard a round of applause and saw that the first gymnast in my line had finished and her score was being flashed — 7.2. I watched the next two, and the best score was 8.5. Then it was my turn.

The head judge signaled for me to start, and I signaled back, which is what Tomo had told us to do. He said that one of the dumbest things you can do is start when the judges aren't looking.

The music was playing, and miraculously as soon as I started my butterflies settled down, and I floated through my routine. I knew it went well, because my main concern had been connections, and everything flowed together. I heard the applause, and went to the section of the bleachers where the contestants wait their turn. Tomo was there and as I sat down next to him, he said, "That was terrific."

"Thanks," I said, and then eagerly looked at the scoring pole. It seemed to take forever, and I watched as a little kid, who was one of the runners, raced over to the scoring table. Finally my score was flashed — 9.05. There was a lot of applause, but it could have been for the other gymnasts, as well as for me, since four events were going on at the same time. Jeanne, who had just finished her routine on the beam came over to me, all smiles, and said, "Super."

I knew she was referring to my score, and I couldn't stop smiling either. I kept saying to myself *I've got to keep it up!*

The next event was the bars. That was the one apparatus that could cause me trouble. Sometimes the routine went fine, but not always. I could only hope for the best. I watched as one girl, Number 12, performed on the bars. She looked perfect.

"She's really good," I said to Tomo, tilting my head in her direction.

"You're right," Tomo agreed. "She goes to White Plains High, and her coach told me she's the most promising one in his class."

I didn't say anything, but I think Tomo must have read my mind because he added, "No better than you."

Number 12 had finished her routine and I watched the runner take the judges' score to the scoring table.

"You'll be up soon," Tomo said. "Better chalk up your hands. Good luck."

"I'll need it," I mumbled, and headed for the chalk box which was located near the bars. All the time I kept my eye on the scoring pole to see what Number 12 had earned. Then I saw her total flashed: 9.15, and I knew I could never do as well. I said to myself that I wasn't really in competition with anyone — but still. Then I forced myself to stop worrying about anyone else's score, and focus on what I was doing.

When I received the signal to begin from the judge, I indicated I was ready with a nod of my head, poised myself, and went through my routine. It went okay, without any major goofs, but I felt it was a little sloppy. I returned to the bleachers and waited. At last my score was flashed and it was 8.75 — better than I expected.

Tomo said, "You're doing fine. Hang in there."

"At least the worst is over for me. The bars are the hardest."

"You scored well. Nothing to worry about." Tomo was always sincere, and he did renew my confidence.

The vault was next and that was the routine I felt most secure in. I knew it went well and I scored a 9.

My last event was the beam. That was the one exercise I had practiced endlessly at home and since I was no longer afraid of the height, I figured I would make my highest score here. There was always the possibility that I'd blow the whole thing by not mounting properly, or wobbling once I was up, but I tried not to worry about that.

When it was my turn, I took a deep breath and began. Once I was into it, I stopped thinking about everything — even the fact that what seemed like a million people were watching me. When I'd finished and returned to my seat next to Tomo, he shook his head in amazement. "It's got to be close to a 10," he said beaming. I knew he wouldn't kid about something like that and all I could do was hope. Then again it seemed to take an eternity before the runner took my score from the judge to the scoring table. The total flashed and the pole slowly turned so that everyone could see — 9.20. There was a roar from the crowd, and Tomo pressed my arm. He'd been keeping his own calculations, and he looked at them briefly. "Congratulations!" he shouted. "You'll definitely qualify for the state, and you'll automatically be in Class II."

I tried to hide my excitement, otherwise I'd be jumping up and down. Jeanne came over to us and said, "It's over. Now all we have to do is wait for the others to finish. Thank goodness." Then she squeezed my shoulder and said, "You were terrific."

For the first time in my life, I knew what it

meant to be speechless. I honestly couldn't say a word. I watched the other contestants in a daze, but I could hardly see them. And then everyone finished performing and drifted over to the bleachers to wait for the results. The gymnasts were asking each other "How d'ja do? Did you qualify for the sectional?" One little pigtailed kid was in tears, and an older girl was trying to comfort her, saying, "You can always try again," but Pigtails couldn't stop sobbing.

Then finally the official at the scoring table said in his sonorous voice, "Attention, please. We now have the all-around scores for the contestants and they will be posted on the bulletin board next to the office. I will announce the six top winners, beginning with sixth place. Please hold your applause until the end." He spoke slowly and distinctly and paused between each total so long that I didn't think he'd ever get finished. Number 33, 28.5; Number 5, 29; Number 24, 31.8; Number 36, 32.5; Number 12, 35.5; Number 18, 36.

There was thunderous applause from the audience and the next few minutes were like a dream. I don't know how I got there, but I found myself almost in the center of the gym floor, surrounded by people. I vaguely remember Tomo tossing me up into the air and shouting, "You've done it! You've done it!"

Everyone seemed to want to get near me and touch me. E.J. was actually crying and smiling at the same time. She flung her arms around me and cried, "Honey, you were magnificent."

Her friend was just behind her and I could hear Phyllis saying, "E.J., you've got some super athlete for a daughter." For some reason, that stuck in my mind. I never really thought of myself as a "super" anything, but I'd never forget those words, and E.J.'s response: "You're telling me! She's terrific!"

Then Carolyn, who actually had tears in her eyes, gave me a quick hug. "I'm so proud of you," she said. "I now have a famous kid sister."

Before I could say anything, Carolyn was pushed aside, and Ellen, and Jackie, and Tracy, on her crutches, had made a circle around me and started to cheer: "Hip, hip, hooray, this is Lizo's day! Hip, hip, hooray, this is Lizo's day!"

The photographer for the school newspaper was taking pictures, and bulbs started flashing. Now, not only couldn't I talk, but for a few seconds I couldn't see!

Then my father was in front of me. Instinctively I ran into his outstretched arms and buried my head in his chest. I don't know how long we stayed like that, but when he finally released me I could see he was trying hard not to show his emotion. His eyes were glistening and he said in a raspy voice, "Congratulations!"

I knew he wanted to say so much more, and I wanted to say so much too — to let him know that without his encouragement from the very beginning none of this would have happened. If he hadn't run interference with E.J., and played down my bleeding hands, and shared with me his feelings about winning a gold medal, I never would have had this triumph. But I could barely speak. I knew he understood that, even though all I managed to say was, "Thank you."

"My turn," I heard Roger say as he pushed his way through the crowd. He put his hands on my shoulders and kissed me in front of everyone. Then he whispered in my ear, "I told you it was worth it."